Seven Dogs
In Heaven

by

Angelo Dirks
Leland Dirks

Illustrations by AugieDoggy.com

ISBN: 1466352752
ISBN-13: 978-1466352759

DEDICATION

This book is dedicated to my late friend Matthew Ketterman, and to all who wear or have worn the uniform of service to this country. .

CONTENTS

ACKNOWLEDGMENTS

When I was a little boy and dreamed of being a writer, it sounded like the most perfect job in the world. Quiet, solitary, and methodical. As an adult who is actually earning his living by writing, I know that nothing could be further from the truth. It turns out that putting a book out there for the world to read is one of the most collaborative processes known to mankind.

I'd like to thank those that collaborated in this effort.

First, the brilliant illustrations are by AugieDoggy.com. I was stunned by the kind offer to do them, and I am stunned at their beauty and simplicity. I am grateful for Augie and Ti's support and patience, while the illustrator did her work. Go check out their website!

Second, may we have a huge round of applause for NPR's Three Minute Fiction staff. They are part of the Weekend All Things Considered staff, and it was through their contest that I found the motivation to try writing again. It was also through that contest that I met some of the most thoughtful and creative writers I've ever known.

Next, yes, go ahead, stand up and take a bow; these are the people who took my ramblings and ideas and pointed out where some polishing was needed, where a few commas might be saved, and where the words or ideas made no sense. They not only did all of that, but each day they inspire me with their own lives and writing. Thank you to Randy Austin, Joan Childs, Laurie Crist, Elizabeth Heath, Sherry Ketterman, Navin Madras, Caroline Nash, Amy Redd-Greiner, Lisa Rouse, and Emma Saunders Tyre.

The next folks I'd like to thank are those wonderful people who sell books. The publishing industry is in turmoil right now, and the folks who are bearing the brunt of it are the booksellers. Even with their world turning upside down, some brave independent bookstore owners took a chance on carrying our first book, Angelo's Journey. Please patronize them, and help keep them around. Even if they don't have a book in stock, they can get it for you. Special thanks to these bookstores who took a chance on an unknown author: Lazy Lion Books in Fuquay-Varina, NC; The Tattered Cover in Denver, CO; Elliott Bay Book Company in Seattle, WA; Moby Dickens Bookshop in Taos, NM; The Avid Reader in Davis, CA; and the Fort Garland Museum Gift Shop in Fort Garland, CO.

For advice on Bach and the music mentioned in the book, and for lending me his Border Collie's name, I am grateful to Tomasz Mońko. If you don't know about his incredible photographs or his beautiful organ music, look him up on Facebook. I think he has the soul of a Border Collie himself.

Thanks, too, to Angelo and Maggie, my fearless and faithful canine companions who learned the phrase "in a minute" could mean "forever" unless whining and cold noses were used to their fullest advantage. My dogs, current and past, have taught me more than I can say. God blessed me greatly when He brought them into my life.

And last but most certainly not least, tail wags and thank you to each of you who make it possible for me to write. Your purchase of my books feeds not only my spirit but also my body and my dogs' bodies. You are truly wonderful and kind, and we couldn't do it without you. Your words of praise, your reviews, your encouragement, and your suggestions on how I can improve all mean the world to the dogs and to me.

1 THE END

Lonely men who live with dogs do the most peculiar things. They begin by talking to their canine friends. Over time, they come to believe their dogs understand them. Eventually, they even believe that they understand what their dogs are saying.

The man thought this as he shivered in the snow. He wished again that his cell phone were in his pocket instead of on the charger at home. He heard his dog running through the saplings at the creek.

The winter sun edged closer to the horizon. The air grew colder.

What an idiot. I knew my hip hurt, but I didn't think it would make me stumble down the creek bank.

53 years old. Not old enough to be crippled, but not young enough to have as much self-confidence as he'd felt this morning.

I wonder if anyone will notice I'm missing?

His hand touched his leg where it bent at an improbable angle, the source of his blinding pain. He looked around at the marks in the snow where he had earlier tried to pull himself up the creek bank.

What would it be like to die this way?

They say that freezing to death is a good way to go. First you get a little sleepy, then a lot sleepy, then you sleep, and then you die.

Will I dream?

Dreams had gotten him into this. He'd always dreamt of building a home in the middle of nowhere. He had spent nearly four years doing exactly that. His closest neighbors were miles away, and he saw them infrequently.

His dog had more of a social life than he did. Angelo, his old-souled Border Collie, patrolled an astonishing range.

As the winter light grew grayer and shadows lengthened, he heard the dog approaching. Angelo held the carcass of a cottontail rabbit in his mouth. The dog brought it closer, so the man could reach it.

So, my friend, you weren't playing at all. You were hunting. Thank you.

The man winced as he pulled a knife from his pocket and began cutting the rabbit into parts.

The first piece went to Angelo, the hunter. Steam left the nostrils of the dog's white-striped nose as he took his due.

The man looked at the next piece, remembering the warnings about parasites in uncooked rabbit. He laughed. Parasites didn't stand a chance in his cold body.

He put the raw meat in his mouth and chewed.

He cut another piece for Angelo, and still another for himself. The last went to Angelo who gnawed the bones appreciatively.

Angelo curled up next to the man. Their two hearts found a common rhythm. Angelo rested his chin on the man's neck.

The man looked at him, smiling at the pack the two of them made. Was it only his imagination or had Angelo become more human and he more canine?

The man's eyes grew heavy. He felt Angelo's warm tongue wash his face. Gravity won the battle for his eyelids as he closed his mind to the pain of his broken leg.

When they found the man's body a week later, they noticed the hollow in the snow by his chest, where something had been lying. His face was clear of snow. They saw an icicle at one eye.

They never found the dog, but the old timers will tell you that the next spring, some of the coyote pups had white stripes on their noses.

2 IMAGINATION

"Heaven goes by favor. If it went by merit, you would stay out and your dog would go in."
—Mark Twain

I awoke that morning to the smell of sagebrush, wood smoke, and frying bacon. My eyes opened to a blue sky with no clouds. My first thought was, "Where's Angelo?"

My second thought was, "Where am I?"

I looked around as I sat up and realized my leg didn't hurt. Though still in the same creek bed where I had fallen asleep, the snow was gone. Spring was in the air, but where was the smell of bacon coming from?

Then I saw him; not Angelo, but a German Shorthaired Pointer with a spatula in his hand. In his paw, I mean. He looked my way, grinned, and offered a cheery "Guten Morgen."

I must be losing my mind. Now I'm dealing with a German-speaking dog I don't know. I looked at him again. His liver-and-white colored fur shined brightly in the morning sun. His brown eyes looked deep into mine. Something about him was familiar. I decided to greet him in his own language. "Sprechen Sie Englisch?" If this phrase didn't work, I'd be reduced to asking for Sauerkraut, the only other German word I knew.

"Ja. I speak English. Probably speak it better than you. I was just messin' with ya." His abrupt change in language and accent was more than a little unnerving.

"Where's Angelo? Have you seen him?"

"He'll be along, give him time."

"And who are you, and why are you here?" I stood up, gingerly testing my weight on my now apparently unbroken leg. "And where *is* here, anyway?"

"Aw, you hurt my feelin's. Really? You don't recognize li'l ole me? I was figgerin' that you'd know me right off." He stopped, tipped his head, and deepened his stare. "Still don't recognize me?"

"Hey, wait a minute. Are you Scout?"

He smiled with his tail and returned his attention to the frying pan, masterfully flipping the eggs over.

"Scout. Um, I'm surprised to see you."

"Really? Why are you surprised?" His ears perked in canine question marks.

Was I hallucinating? Dreaming? I decided to play along. "Well, let's see. How do I say this respectfully? Scout, you aren't real. I mean, you may be real here, but I made you up. You're a character in a story I wrote."

"Real, schmeal. As soon as you imagined me, I was real. As soon as you put me into that book, *Angelo's Journey*, I began to breathe and belch and, well, you know. I'm still a little annoyed that you killed me off in the story, but hey, I don't hold grudges. Not for very long, anyway."

"It could've been worse. I could have just left you hanging with the Wildman you lived with."

"Ja. That would have been worse."

"That bacon smells wonderful. Is it ready yet?"

Scout shook his head. "One minute I'm not real, the next he wants me to hurry up with breakfast. Make up your mind, human."

"Okay, okay. You're real. At least until breakfast is done."

"So help out a little. Go over to that china hutch," he gestured with the spatula, "get the dishes, and set the table."

I looked where he pointed the spatula, and sure enough, there was a china hutch, a dining table, and two chairs where there had been only grass before. A red and white checked tablecloth rippled in the gentle breeze.

"Hurry, already!"

By the time I turned from the china hutch to the table, Scout had put the frying pan on a trivet, and the coffee pot was on the table, too. A pitcher of syrup and steaming hotcakes completed the picture.

"Coffee cups, too. The big mugs. And no, I don't take cream or sugar and neither do you."

He was right.

"Silverware. In the drawers. Hurry! It's all getting cold!"

Folded white linen napkins had appeared by the time I got the silver.

"Eat!"

"We don't say grace in heaven? I mean, this is heaven, right?"

"I just did. EAT! This road to heaven stuff makes a lost soul hungry! Time for questions later!"

And eat we did. Scout had the best table manners I'd seen since I had eaten in the elegant Brennan's restaurant in New Orleans. He knew which fork to use, which knife, and he was gracious enough to keep topping off my coffee and filling my plate with more pancakes and bacon. Throughout the whole breakfast, it seemed as if he could read my mind, serving whatever I wanted. My remembering Brennan's reminded me of beignets, which appeared out of nowhere, and slid onto my plate.

I can't say I had my fill, as it seemed I could eat forever without feeling overfull, but eventually I grew tired of eating, and Scout knew it. His brown eyes looked at my hazel eyes for confirmation, and I nodded. His good manners must have rubbed off on me, because I offered to help clean up.

"Pshaw. We'll let the cats clean off the plates and I'll clean the rest up later." Right on cue, a pair of gray cats jumped on the table and attacked the remaining bacon and eggs. They saved the sticky syrup from the pancakes for last.

"That was wonderful! My compliments to the chef!"

"If I'd had a little more time I could have whipped up some crêpes, but we make do with what we have. Let's go sit by the creek and talk. Bring your coffee."

We walked, me on two legs, him on four. I had seen no creek, but of course, Scout was right. The dappled shade from the grove of aspen trees (which also hadn't been there earlier) made the water shimmer in a most inviting way. The creek's gurgly voice filled the air.

"Okay, now you can ask me questions." Scout bobbed his head as he slurped water from the clear running creek, reverting to the manners I would expect from a dog.

"Well, maybe one or two." I didn't add the word "million" though it certainly was in my mind.

Scout stretched out on the green grass, and I laid myself down so that we were eye-to-eye. "How'd you get here? How'd I get here? I mean, at least I am—was—real. I thought—"

He interrupted, "We're back to real, huh? Okay, let's talk a little about real and imagination first. You humans, you teach your pups—children—not to run with scissors but you don't teach them anything about the power or the danger of imagination."

I must have looked confused. Or discombobulated. At least disbelieving.

Shaking his head just enough to make his ears flop, he continued, "Okay, let's take it from the top. When you were a kid, you wanted to be a grown-up, right? You imagined it with every fiber of your being. You stopped *imagining* that you would grow up and you *believed* you would grow up. Am I right?"

"Well, I suppose so. But I knew that was going to happen." I was getting a little shaky on his logic.

"And that is my point. When imagination changes from hoping to knowing, it makes things real." He looked as hopefully at me as I had looked at every dog I ever told, "I've got to work but I'll be home later." Something like, "Dear God, I hope he gets this simple concept."

"But if imagination can do that, then what's real?"

Scout nodded, as if he were a teacher dealing with a student who had finally understood the Pythagorean theorem. "Exactly!"

"But I imagined myself being a cowboy, too. And a fireman. And—"

"But you didn't believe. You thought those sounded cool, but you didn't truly believe."

I considered his words. Of course he was right. I didn't completely believe that I would be a cowboy or a fireman. I knew I'd get away from the farm I grew up on and move to the city, to seek the arts, the "in" places, and the popular people. A desk job in a big city was the most exciting thing I could imagine. And that's exactly what I'd had for 25 years.

"So does imagination work slowly?"

"Sometimes it works slowly, sometimes it works quickly. Here I am, a Pointer. Imagine me as a Chihuahua with a Santa Claus hat."

I blinked my eyes, and there he was, looking like a Mexican fast food holiday card.

"It's not always so easy. It takes more energy to imagine for yourself than for others. As a matter of fact, it's very easy to imagine for other people. Other beings. Think of all those homeless people you used to walk by, calling them failures. What do you suppose became of them?" His voice was now annoyingly yippy. High pitched. Like a, well, like a Chihuahua. I blinked again, and he was back to the German Shorthaired Pointer I'd almost grown accustomed to.

His voice, too, returned to normal. Whatever normal was. "And the reality only lasts as long as you truly believe, as long as you *know*."

I hated feeling his judgment. Almost as much as I hated the responsibility I was feeling for all the people I'd imagined as

7

zeroes, nothings, nobodies. All the homeless dogs I'd assumed would be euthanized.

The silence was long. My introspection was deep. "So why don't they warn us? Why don't they teach us about the power of imagination?"

"That, my human friend, is a mystery to me. You see, I can't fathom why humans do much of what they do, or why they don't do what they don't do. There are, of course, exceptions. We have hope because of those few."

I felt only doubt.

"Are you going to tell me what happened to Angelo?"

"He'll be along. He's not going to forget you. Now, I believe I am going to imagine it is night. I think your first day here has held enough surprises." And with that, the bright sunlight faded to the dark blue of dusk. I thought about lighting a fire. With my imagination. But my eyes were heavy, and I soon fell into a restless sleep, with an invented dog at my feet. In one final act of imagination, I *knew* he didn't snore.

#######

In the shadows, Nicholas Beales, Esq., witnessed the scene and spoke to himself: "Sssuch a misssfit. Easssy cassse." He would have rubbed his hands together in glee, if he had had hands

.

3 LOYALTY

"His name is not wild dog anymore, but the first friend, because he will be our friend for always and always and always."
—Rudyard Kipling, Indian-born British author (1865-1936)

I gradually came awake in a meadow. Before I was aware of anything else, I felt the empty space beside me, a space Angelo should have filled. I smelled the freshness of the grass, and I felt the warmth of the sun on my skin. A creek laughed in the distance. Still groggy, I felt something rough and wet on my face.

I'd know that sensation anywhere. Canine tongue. A dog was licking my face. I opened my eyes, and there was a familiar English Shepherd, standing guard over me. I smiled, and rubbed her chin. She smiled back at me.

No matter how often we bathed her, Trixie always carried just a hint of the persistent and pungent odor of skunk. She was a fierce protector, not only of me but also of Mom's chickens. But the skunks kept trying.

I sat up, and was overwhelmed by the millions of glistening diamonds of dew on the grass. Yellow blossoms punctuated the carpet of sparkling green. Trixie put one paw on my shoulder and licked my ear.

"Thank goodness you're finally awake! I was starting to worry."

"I had the strangest dream. I…" I looked over my shoulder, trying to find the source of the crystalline voice that had expressed concern. It was a voice that sounded like a summer rainstorm pattering on single pane windows.

But it was just the dog and me. Puzzled, I realized I must have hit my head harder than I thought. Wait, when did I hit my head? *Did* I hit my head?

"You poor thing. You're just a little confused, aren't you?" The xylophonic voice was definitely hers.

"Wait, what are you doing here? You're dead! Dad put you down because you had distemper!"

Trixie's dark brown eyes met mine. "You're dead, too, my friend. Don't you remember falling asleep in the snow? Do you remember the dream?"

"There was this dog. Scout. I wrote a story about him."

"Oh, yes, he's quite the trickster. He explained to you about how things work up here?"

"Um, he explained a lot, but I wouldn't mind hearing your version. So I'm really dead?"

"Oh, dear. He was supposed to talk to you about 'really.' And yes, dear, you're dead. I know. It was a shock when it happened to me, too. Give yourself a little time to get used to it."

Dead. Heaven, maybe. "So, is this heaven?"

"Well," her voice tinkled, "It's a little more complicated than that. You humans always try to make things too simple, except when you're trying to make things too complicated. You can never just *be* with what *is*."

Her brown eyes looked at me in pity; the special pity reserved for someone who was a little too dull to cross the street alone.

Trying not to feel like a child, I asked in my most adult voice, "Are you going to tell me where Angelo is?"

"Why don't we play for a while? I brought one of your favorite toys," she said as she turned away from my question. I followed her gaze, and there was my wagon. My red, rusty, trusty Radio Flyer wagon. But it wasn't rusty any more. It was as shiny as the day I got it for my fourth birthday. Its black handle glistened in the early morning sun, and its race-car-red body glowed. If it had had an engine, it would have been revving.

I looked back at Trixie. Somehow, she'd slipped into the crude rope harness I'd made for her when I was a kid, and she loped toward the wagon.

I stood up, feeling a little dizzy. Maybe a lot dizzy. But the dizziness came from confusion and wonder and amazement, not from any injury.

My feet were bare, and the wet grass tickled my toes. In the time I walked to the wagon, Trixie had attached the harness to the wagon handle.

"Let's go!" She laughed.

I got in the wagon, which somehow accommodated my grown-up body without any discomfort. Odd, since I remembered the wagon being too small for me when I put it away for the last time. What was I, ten?

"Wait. You're here. The wagon's here. I'm here. But where *is* here?"

Trixie began pulling me, slowly at first, and then picking up speed, all the while ignoring my questions.

"You're not going to answer my questions, are you?"

"Just hush and enjoy yourself!"

I surrendered and closed my eyes. The wind of motion flowed over my cheeks. It was a gentle breeze but grew to be gale force. The sound of Trixie's feet padding through the grass changed to clicking a split second before the quiet wheels of the wagon changed timbre to reveal that we were now on a gravel road.

Faster and faster Trixie ran. My eyes opened again and saw the sunflowers at the sides of the road blurring into yellow lines. After a long while, she slowed down, coming to a complete stop at an old-fashioned covered bridge.

"Time to get out and walk. I'm not going to take you everywhere, you lazy human." She slipped the harness from her shoulders and waited patiently for me to get out of the wagon.

I braced myself for my creaky knees to complain at being bent for so long, but my legs unfolded without complaint, and I stood without a single pop from my old joints.

"What's happened? Did I get a new body when I died? I'm going to take better care of this one."

"No you won't. You'll walk too far, you'll forget to eat, and you'll have more wine than you probably should. At least now, you'll self-heal. Speaking of wine, I put some in the backpack for later."

Backpack? I wasn't sure how it got there, but I felt a backpack strap across my shoulder. It wasn't heavy, but I could smell fresh-baked bread, and I heard wine glasses clinking against each other. I was starting to like this life after death stuff.

"Good!" Trixie roused me from my reverie. "Now you're starting to do what you should do. Be here. Be now. No book of philosophy ever made a loaf of bread smell better."

She loped alongside the creek and I kept up even as she broke into a trot. Still the grass tickled the bottoms of my feet.

"Ah, here we are." Trixie sat down on her haunches, and looked expectantly at me. "Why don't you open the backpack and get the blanket out, and we'll eat."

Looking at the long grass around us, I hesitated and then asked, "Is it safe? I mean, are there any snakes here?"

Her laughter changed her voice from wind chimes to the jingling of sleigh bells. She clutched at her stomach, and rolled over in the grass. She laughed until tears came to her eyes.

"Let me get this straight. You died of hypothermia, you're alive again in the most beautiful place you've ever imagined, you're accompanied by your long dead childhood dog, and you're worried that a snake might hurt you?"

Sheepishly, I sat down in the grass, and opened the backpack. "You don't have to be sarcastic about it."

"Sorry, it's just…" Her peals of laughter once again poured forth. Finally getting hold of herself, she apologized. "It's just that, well, I haven't run into many humans lately, and you all are the best sources of jokes. Snakes! Ha! Wait till I tell the others!"

Resisting my initial urge to ask about the snake in the Garden of Eden, I seized upon the mention of "others" as a way to change the direction of the conversation. Perhaps even salvage a little of my battered dignity.

"Others? Yes, why haven't we run into any others?"

"Oh, well, everyone's very busy. Much work to be done. You'll meet the others soon enough."

"And Angelo?"

"All in good time. Now, would you get the wine and glasses out of the backpack? And the corkscrew?"

I reached into the backpack, retrieved a bottle of South African Shiraz of excellent vintage, and found two very fragile Lalique wine goblets. I must be in heaven, or these thousand dollar glasses would be in pieces. Trixie took the bottle in her paws, put it on the blanket, and waited somewhat impatiently for me to locate the corkscrew. "Oh, here it is. Here you go."

She took the corkscrew from my hand, spun it into the cork, and popped the cork out. Amazing. More amazing because I didn't realize how amazing it was until she began pouring the wine into the goblets.

"How'd you do that?"

"Oh, we canines are quite resourceful. All that talk of opposable thumbs was barking up quite the wrong tree. We acted helpless to see if you'd come to our rescue."

She continued her monologue. "Know what I really wish I'd had? A way to carry more than one thing at a time. Backpacks. Pockets. Purses. Imagine the complications of carrying one thing at a time, having to find a safe place for it, and then remembering where you put it. It slowed the progress of the canine race horribly, until we trained you humans."

"You trained us?"

"Well, duh. Who was it that went to work every day, carried the groceries in, and scrubbed the floors? Who was it that took naps and watched Animal Planet every day? Oh sure, we had to time our bodily functions to match your schedule, but all in all, it gave us more time to meditate and pray."

Trixie took a moment to have a sip of wine. "You poor dears. You just didn't understand." Her eyes seemed to be focused on the blanket. "Sometimes, some of you had such moments of clarity. You'd see a two-footer or a four-footer in need, and you'd help. You'd see a hungry face and you'd try to feed it. But there were so many others who didn't."

The tinkling of her voice took on a tone more like a church bell tolling after a funeral.

"I don't get it, Trixie, why are you bringing all this up now?"

Her stare shifted to my eyes. "We shared lives, not as a test, but as a chance to learn from each other." Again she paused. "It's still a puzzle to me what we dogs were supposed to learn from you humans. Still a puzzle. But it was clear from the start what we could teach you. Unconditional love. Trust. Loyalty. Especially loyalty."

She looked me hard in the eye. "Do you remember when you got lost in the wheat fields? Your mother was frantic. You were just a little bit shorter than the stalks of wheat. You had wandered off, and no one knew which direction you had gone."

My mind filled with that day. The smell of rain-washed stalks of wheat again infused my nostrils. A dense forest of tall grassy blades reaching toward the heavens. Mashing down wheat plants enough to make a bed so that I could watch the clouds in the sky making shapes of impossible animals. "I do remember."

"Two miles your little toddler legs carried you. Your mother was so afraid. She tried to follow your footprints in the soil, but you had crossed the hard road and she lost your trail. For hours she cried your name, but in the wrong direction. I walked with her at first, dismayed by her poor sense of smell. She reached down to pet me and call me 'good dog.' I decided that she would be all right on her own, and I followed your scent down the road and into that wheat field. The fear of snakes you have now? I had it then, and that field had a lot of rattlesnakes. But I kept following your scent until I found you.

"You were napping. You looked up at the sky when I finally got you awake. You smiled at me until I grabbed the collar of your shirt in my jaws and made you stand up. Your little hand held on to my fur so tightly it hurt, but that was a small price to pay as I led you to safety. I'll never forget your mother running over to you, hugging you tight, and making sure you were all right."

I pondered. "And you were teaching me loyalty through all of that?" I saw my hand clutching her fur now, as she told the story.

"Loyalty. Yes. Facing frightening things to save what—and who—is important. Responsibility, too. I should have been watching you that day, but instead, I was napping in the sun when you wandered off."

"Did I learn the lesson?" I asked tenuously.

"That's not for me to say. Do you think you learned the lesson? Did you go out on a limb to help your friends when they needed you most? Did you stick with them when it didn't make sense?"

She let her questions hang there in the still air on the banks of our creek.

Clearing my throat, I answered, "Well, I tried, I guess. So I guess the lessons stuck."

"Like I said, that's not for either of us to judge. Now, break open that loaf of bread and put some cheese on it. I'm rather partial to the Brie, myself."

She let the serious talk slide for a while, and we spent time reminiscing about the good old days. She filled in some gaps in my memories for me.

"So whatever happened to my G.I. Joe?"

"Your brother took it. He took a Barbie doll from your friend Paula, too."

"But why? I would have let him play with it."

"Let's just say even in those days he had an, um, active imagination about the things males and females do together."

"What about my red Matchbox car?"

"Oh. Well, I'm afraid that's my fault."

"Trixie, you want to tell me the story?"

"Well, in those days I was a—how shall I say it—a less enlightened being. I was jealous. I buried it. I wanted your attention to be on me, not some little toy. But here. I dug it up and made it all new again."

And in my hands was that little red Ford Galaxy 500, candy apple red. No longer than a finger. Shiny. New.

I was starting to like, and believe in, this life after death stuff. But still I missed my Border Collie.

#######

A pair of unblinking eyes watched this interchange. "Sssuch arrogance. 'The lessssons sssstuck.' Ssstupid imbecile. Sssuch certainty is ssssadly misssplaced."

4 DUTY

"A dog is not considered a good dog because he is a good barker. A man is not considered a good man because he is a good talker."
—Chuan-Tzu, Chinese sage, (ca. 250 BC)

It was almost a routine now. Each day, I woke up in a place and time different from where I fell asleep. The only constant was my longing for Angelo's warm paw on my shoulder to wake me up.

That day, when I opened my eyes, I saw not a cloud in the blue sky. The eastern horizon consisted of my beloved Sangre de Cristo mountain range. To the west, however, where the San Juan mountains should be, there were rolling fields of wheat, ready to turn the color of harvest. The wind rippled the heads of wheat, like waves on a golden ocean. Somewhere, I heard the creek gurgle.

"Remind you of home?" A gruff voice came from behind me. Before I even looked, I knew who it had to be. It was Snowboy.

His long white fur was pristine, not the dirty gray I remembered from all those years ago. His eyes, one blue, one brown, seemed to have grown clearer since then, too.

He spoke, "Well, are you going to lie here all day?"

"No, sir!" I exclaimed as I stood up. Something was different today, something about my body. I glanced down at my lower body. Good Lord, I was wearing those awful red hip hugger pants from when I was what, seven? I was shorter, too. Just about the height I was when I was—seven. Oh, God, please don't make me go through puberty again.

"So, you do remember me," the stern voice stated more than asked. "You didn't forget me after all."

We stood together in companionable silence as I remembered this dog. His name wasn't really Snowboy; it was Snowball. But when I was small, I couldn't say "ball" so I said something that sounded like "Snowboy," and the name stuck.

He wasn't a pup when he came to us; he was full grown. Grandma's neighbors, Faye and Walt, moved from their farm into town, and Faye didn't think Snowboy would adapt. A Chow-Pomeranian mix, Grandma's friend called him. Long hair, long teeth, the only thing he wasn't long on was patience.

"So you're remembering how it was?" His voice, it suddenly came to me, was remarkably like my father's.

"Yeah, how you came to us. What you were like."

"I wonder how well you knew me. I wonder if you know what it's like to vow to protect a family and then to be given away like so much unwanted baggage."

I looked down at the ground as his words sank in. I compared his experiences with my own. I, too, had been disowned by my family.

"Yeah, I think I can understand. But I never thought of it that way. For you, I mean. I mean, you were just a—"

"Just a dog, you were going to say? Yeah, I was 'just a dog.'"

"I didn't mean it like that. I—"

"You meant it exactly like that. Don't lie."

He was right. I'd resented him back then. He wasn't anything like Trixie. There was no play in this big fluffy dog. Just fierceness.

"I know I was hard on you. When you wanted to dress me up, I stayed just out of reach of your sticky little hands. When you wanted me to pull you around in that wagon, I growled. Well, it's time for you to know why."

"Okay, I'm listening."

"You all thought I was well-behaved by nature. It wasn't that way. When I was a pup, I chewed on everything. I chewed a tire right off a tractor.

"Times were different back then. People made us dogs stay outside in winter and summer. I got bored easily. That happens to those of us with brains. You might know something about that. Maybe.

"When Walt came out that morning and saw that he was missing a tire on his tractor, he had his belt out of his pants and whipping through the air before I could move." His eyes watered.

"That was my last day of play. I was afraid they'd throw me out, stop feeding me, stop loving me. I promised myself and God that I would work every day, as hard as I could. I'd protect them, I'd herd for them, I'd warn them about the things I couldn't handle on my own. I'd do my duty."

Snowboy shifted on his feet and stared at me, the blue eye focusing hard on me, the brown eye looking into the distance. "I kept that promise, and what happened? They dumped me on you and your family. How was I supposed to feel?"

I remembered the day that Faye and Walt brought Snowboy and his ramshackle doghouse to our farm. I even remembered the look of terror and anger in his eyes when they got back in their pickup truck and drove off without him. He howled in pain. He kept howling for a week.

"I howled until I was hoarse. I waited at the end of your driveway. Your mom brought me food and water. Do you remember what you did?"

19

Hot blood flowed to my ears. "Yes," I said in a voice barely above a whisper.

"What? I couldn't hear you."

"Yes," I nearly shouted. "I told you to shut up. I couldn't stand your whining any more."

"Do you remember what happened?"

"You did shut up. Almost immediately."

"What you won't remember is what didn't happen. I didn't bite you. Instead, I renewed my promise to God to protect my family. My new family. And I prayed that you wouldn't kick me or whip me. That I wouldn't be given away again.

"So, again, I did my duty. I protected you. I was glad you didn't have cattle or sheep. I hated the smell of those stupid animals. I warned you of any dangers I couldn't handle."

And then, he almost smiled.

I guessed why he smiled and prompted him. "Like the propane man?"

"Hey, how did I know he wasn't trying to do something bad?"

I was relieved. It felt like his monologue was nearly over. "I get your point. I'm sorry I wasn't nicer to you. I didn't know, didn't understand. I was just a—"

"Just a boy? Yeah, you were."

I made as if to stand up and felt his stare again. "What?"

"We're not done yet."

I settled back down. "Oh."

The silence grew long. The only sound was the creek, and even it seemed subdued. I waited.

"Do you remember the last day? My last day?"

My ears, so recently hot with shame went suddenly cold with dread. I nodded.

His eyes were no longer on me. They stared into a space that was some forty years ago. "You wanted to go on a hike. Just a mile or so away, but it was the first time you'd walk to that locust tree, in the middle of that golden sea of wheat. Your mom insisted I go with you. She knew I'd protect you. She packed a lunch for us. Bologna for me, peanut butter and jelly for you.

And a jug of water. You brought books. You wanted to read on that glorious summer day. I never did understand why you always had your nose in a book."

I picked up the story. "I put it all into my little red wagon. You watched me like you didn't trust me."

"I didn't trust you. It was my duty to watch you."

"I pulled the wagon. I knew by then you sure weren't going to do it. I pulled the wagon up the quarter-of-a-mile driveway all by myself."

"You were young. You'd never been that far alone, at least not with permission. Your mom or your brothers were always with you. But I'd waited there. I'd watched the cars and trucks go by. I'd waited there that first week, and I'd waited there every time your family got into your red car and drove away. Anyway, you didn't understand roads or how to cross them. Ninety-nine days out of a hundred, no one else would have been on that road. But that day—" Snowboy paused.

I continued the story, "But that day there was someone else on that road. I was reading a book in one hand while I pulled the wagon with the other. You got weird. You bit my leg."

He interrupted. "I tried to push you into the ditch, out of the way. You wouldn't listen. I had to bite. Still you wouldn't listen. Finally I pushed you until you fell into the ditch."

"I fell into the ditch and you got run over by that truck." Tears blurred my vision. I couldn't go on.

I felt his chin on my shoulder. I sobbed. "I'm sorry. I'm so sorry." My arm wrapped around Snowboy, my hands grasped that deep, soft fur. "Please forgive me."

I felt him pull back. "Boy, you've got a lot to learn up here. Do you remember what you did after the truck hit me and kept going?"

My memory was blank after the thud of metal hitting fur. I shook my head.

"You crawled out of the ditch. You looked at me, and you held me. You rocked me for hours until your mom came looking for you. I watched. I had to watch, even after I died. I had to keep my promise."

My sobbing grew erratic. His paw found my shoulder.

"You ask me to forgive you? I'm thanking you. You finally loved me in that moment, and that love set me free, released me from my sworn duty."

We sat there for a long time, boy and dog leaning into each other, in the July-colored sunlight, with the creek singing in a full voice. We were both confident that no one was going to run over either one of us again.

########

A tail slithered in long grass. "Sssso. Sssuch nice thoughtsss. Warmnesssss and cuddlessss. We aren't vanquished sssso easssily, ssstupid sssimpleton. There are legalitiesssss…"

5 LOVE

"Many who have spent a lifetime in it can tell us less of love than the child that lost a dog yesterday."
—Thornton Wilder

I awoke to the unmistakable sound of a tennis ball against a brick wall, echoing throughout whatever place I was this morning. As the cobwebs of sleep receded, I heard something new: a human voice. I hadn't heard one of those since, well, since before I got to this place. Talking dogs didn't sound quite the same as humans.

I opened my eyes. Sunlight streamed in through the windows. These windows I knew; they were in the house I'd lived in for more than 20 years in Denver. As I raised myself up in bed though, I knew I wasn't in Denver. There were no traffic sounds, no exhaust fumes, and the window showed a pasture, not a busy street.

Looking where Angelo would have slept if he had been here made my heart heavy.

I got up and put a robe on, walking down the stairs I'd walked so many times before. The scent and sound of coffee brewing lured me to the kitchen. On the counter was my favorite mug, with Bugs Bunny on the side, so I filled it up and took the first sip. Perfect.

"Hey, Einstein." I turned around to the source of the words. There, with tennis ball in hand, was a clean-cut, all-American guy. One I'd known for years and was proud to call friend.

"Hey, Cowboy. I was wondering when I'd run into you here." How casual I sounded, talking to this man who had died three years ago. Come to think of it, how casual *he* sounded, talking to this guy who died less than a week ago.

We'd met a long time ago. He was a Marine, and he'd fallen in love with my dog. The feeling was mutual. Suki adored him.

Our nicknames came from the first time we met. He was wearing a cowboy hat, and I had used—what did he call it?—a fifty cent word.

I snickered, I hoped to myself.

"What?" he asked with the usual intent look on his face.

"I was just thinking that the song is right. The streets of heaven really are guarded by United States Marines. At least you're here."

He guffawed, "Yeah, I guess so."

I heard the patter of four feet on the floor, and I knew she was here. "Well, for goodness sake. Aren't you going to hug or sniff each other's butts, or whatever it is you humans do to greet each other? Shake hands at least!"

I looked down toward where she stood, and into her almond-shaped eyes as she gestured with them toward Cowboy.

As I awkwardly reached to hug him, he hugged back, and Suki stood against our legs, making for a three-way hug. After only a few moments, our hands bumped into each other on the back of Suki's head, both of us skritching behind her ears.

I may have skipped going through puberty a second time in heaven, but I didn't escape the goose bumps I remembered all too well from the first time I hugged this man.

Finally, our embrace ended. We stepped away from each other and looked each other over, hazel eyes staring into blue eyes, and smiling.

"So, whatcha been up to, Cowboy?"

"Nothin' much, Einstein."

"Been here long?"

"Time flies when you're playing fetch with a Shiba Inu."

"That's more like it," the Japanese dog uttered. "It's good to see you guys together. Together again, I mean."

I looked at her and smiled. Then I dropped to my knees, and she stood on me and licked my face.

Cowboy might be a good hugger, but Suki was the best kisser—at least in quantity, if not quality.

"Girl, I missed you."

"I missed you, too, you big pushover. Figured you could use some human company for a change. I had to pull a few strings you know, to—"

"To get Cowboy to visit?"

"Yeah. You're not really supposed to fraternize with your own species for a while, but the big guy likes me, and he said as long as I chaperoned—"

"You always made the impossible happen, Suki."

"Yeah, you always needed a magician in your life. It was my honor. *Is* my honor."

I regarded her again. The whitish gray I remembered on her nose was gone—it was the same red sesame color as the rest of her fur.

"So there are tennis balls here?"

"Oh yeah, and steaks, and Milk-Bones, and no cars."

Tearing up, I flashed on how I'd lost her to a hit-and-run driver. No cars. Good. I liked that.

I felt Cowboy's light touch on my shoulder. I gave Suki a tickle under the chin and stood up.

"I can't stay real long," Cowboy said. "Like Suki said, it was kind of a special favor."

"But I'll get to see you later?"

"I'd say there's a good chance of that." He paused. "A real good chance."

We stood there a few moments, gawking at each other like awkward teenagers, silly smiles for each other.

"But before I go, I want to say something really clearly that I never said down there."

Gulp.

"What you—and Suki—did for me… I don't think I ever said thanks. When I was in Iraq, those packages of cookies and toilet paper and slobbery tennis balls, well, they got me through some long ugly days. And when I got back and couldn't talk to anyone, the way you listened, without making me feel like I was a murderer, well…"

His eyes, always blue as water, really had water in them now. I jumped in, "Hey, it helped me, too. You mean a lot to me, Cowboy."

He sniffed, like he had an allergic attack or something, and looked me hard in the eyes. "You mean a lot to me, Einstein. Now, I gotta get goin'."

"Already? But I'll see you later, right?"

"If I have anything to say about it, yep. I promise."

And with that, he headed to the door. As his hand reached the knob, he turned back to me and said, "See ya, Einstein."

"Take care, Cowboy."

"Later, Suki!"

And the door closed. Suki laughed.

"Well, 'bout damned time the two of you said something to each other. You humans are a constant source of amazement and frustration to me. You can go on for hours and hours about movies and music and politics, but the word 'love' seems like it's profane or something."

"Yeah, well, sometimes human love is complicated."

"I figured that was one of the greatest gifts we had down on earth. The inability to speak words. Instead, we dogs talked with our actions. Sometimes you humans need to stop talking and thinking so much. You know what's right without all that."

In my heart I knew she was right. But I think I agreed with her: It was a good thing that dogs didn't talk on earth—at least in words. If they did, there'd be a lot of psychiatrists, psychologists, and authors of self-help books out of work.

While one part of my head pondered her words, another was awash with questions. "So you had a hand in getting Angelo to show up at my door, I'm guessing?"

"Oh yeah. You were a mess—"

"Wait, how do you know that? Could you see me?"

"Not really see. Feel. Sense. It's like breathing, or your heart beating. You don't think about it unless something goes wrong. And boy, could I tell stuff was wrong with you. All those thoughts about killing yourself…"

"You know about that?"

"Please. I lived with you for six years. I know everything that goes on in your head."

"Everything? Um…" My face glowed red.

"Yeah, I know everything. But let's pretend I gave you some little bit of privacy." She giggled.

"So another question. When I was sending packages to Cowboy, when he was sent to Iraq, how did you know which one was his? I mean, sometimes there were a dozen packages I was sending to different Marines and soldiers all at once. How did you know which one to drop the pre-slobbered tennis ball into?"

"That was easy. You paused every time you put something in his box. Like you were praying."

Good grief, I'd forgotten how perceptive this dog was. Is. Verb tenses were starting to confuse me.

"Yep. Perceptive. I pay attention. You humans might take a lesson on that. You fill your ears up with noise, spray that funny-smelling stuff all over yourselves, and put blinders on so you only see what you are *supposed to* see. All those shouldas, wouldas, and couldas keep you from seeing what *is*."

We went outside, into what should have been the backyard but was instead yet another meadow bordered by that omnipresent creek on one side. The grass was green, but there wasn't a wildflower or a dandelion to be seen. I laid myself down. Suki settled so that we were facing each other.

"So, Suki, tell me, what should I know about love?"

"You don't believe in starting with easy questions, do you?"

"Please. I'm in the company of a genius Shiba Inu—a *perceptive* Shiba Inu—so I see no reason to start off easy."

"I was thinking more of how complex the answers might be, and your ability to understand them."

"I think I'm insulted."

She blithely ignored my indignation and began, "I am, of course, a recognized expert—"

"And humble?"

"—In love. You sensed that when I chose you. That's why you named me with the Japanese word for love."

I nodded, remembering the day that pup turned her back on her three littermates and raced right over to me.

"Let's start with the easy stuff, the stuff there aren't any good words for. Remember how I laid my head on your lap when we watched TV? And how you skritched between my ears? That was one kind of love. Just being with someone I trusted; someone who knew how to make me feel good; and me doing the same thing for you, just by being with you."

"You never skritched between my ears."

"You know what I mean," she scolded, her eyes taking on a sort of librarian scowl.

"I call that 'puppy love,' and it's a beautiful thing. You with me so far?"

I nodded. "Keeping up. Should I be taking notes?" On the grass in front of me there was a Big Chief tablet and a fat pencil.

Suki continued, "Then let's talk about hero love."

"Hero love?" I was puzzled.

"You know. The kind of love you have for someone you want to be like: Marines, astronauts, cowboys, teachers, big brothers, that sort of thing. You love them because they represent the you that you want to be. Of course, you're disappointed when you discover that they have flaws, because deep down, you know that it means you'll never be perfect either."

"Wait a minute—so you're saying—"

"I'm saying that hero love doesn't usually last very long."

"So, that's bad, right?"

"No, I'm not saying that at all. It serves its purpose. There's not really any kind of love that's 'bad.' All kinds of love teach us about ourselves and about each other."

Picking up the Big Chief tablet, I was prepared to start taking notes when I saw that all of Suki's words had already been written there.

"Cool, huh? You thought I would trust you to write fast enough to keep up?"

I kept my mouth shut. Obviously it was my turn to be a dumb animal.

"Then there's hormone love. The kind where consciousness moves down to your nether regions and your brain goes all stupid." Her words appeared on the tablet as she spoke them.

"And that's not bad, either?"

"In itself, no. You're making me repeat myself, but love itself is never bad. Love is like everything; helpful tool or dangerous weapon, depending on the intent of whoever carries it."

"But—"

"Patience, Grasshopper, only two more to go." Her reference to an old TV show made me laugh.

"Friendship love. This is a very special thing. It's the sort of love where you know another being's strengths and weaknesses, perfections and imperfections, and you love the whole package. We canines are masters of this sort of love."

"Explain please?"

"Think about it. You humans wake up, feed us, maybe take us for a short walk, and then you disappear for eight or ten hours. When you come home, do we resent you and pout? No, we get all excited and kiss you. That's the kind of love that friendship love is."

"One more kind and then I can ask questions?" I have never been particularly good at holding my tongue.

"One more. Big love."

"Big love?" I was torn between looking Suki in the eye and staring at the magic Big Chief tablet that continued to record her words.

"Big love is the kind of love that takes in more than the self. It's love for something bigger than the self. It's love of God, of the universe, of the family, of the pack, of the tribe. It inspires courage and selflessness in those who know it. Now, you had questions?"

"Oh, maybe a few. Maybe one you left out."

Her fuzzy eyebrows raised.

"What about romantic love?"

"Ah, I didn't make this clear. These loves I've defined are rarely separate or discrete. They often grow into one another, blending sometimes. What you call romantic love is a mixture of hero love, friend love, hormone love, and sometimes if you're lucky, big love."

"It's like a recipe?"

"More like an experiment, I think. You keep trying until you get the proportions right. Maybe you start off with hormone love, but add friend love in the morning when you discover each other's laughter. Or maybe after some more time together, you discover a shared desire to help abandoned animals, and so you add big love."

"What about those people who claim that this love or that love is wrong?"

She contemplated. "You have to listen not only to their words but to watch their actions. A lot of them have a sort of hero love gone wrong, and in the worst cases, hormone love that they warp into manipulating people."

"What about the love of money?"

She didn't hesitate at all on this question. "You can't really, truly love a thing. Love is only possible between beings or groups of beings. Love of a thing doesn't work because it can't love back."

In my muddled mind, I kept trying to understand—to believe—that it could be this simple.

She looked at me again with her wise old eyes. "I think that's enough for one day, Grasshopper."

"Just one more question. Cowboy and me. What kind of love do we have?"

Patience radiated from her smile. "I think you have all the information you need to figure that out for yourself."

"But you know?"

"I'm a dog. I know all."

"Except how to be humble?"

She giggled. "Once in a while, there is a little problem with that."

She got up, turned around three times, put her head on my thigh, stretched, and yawned. I yawned, too, and skritched between her ears. The Big Chief tablet wrote no more words. I wanted it to write a note to remind me to ask why dogs turn around three times before they sleep. Perhaps another day. Finally, we slept.

#######

Love and kissssses and sssentimentssss. There are dayssss thisss job isss like nothing sssso much as a sssappy greeting card.

6 PLAY

"The dog was created specifically for children. He is the god of
frolic."
—Henry Ward Beecher

Just one night in a house and I had an expectation of being able
to sleep late. Blinds and curtains could shut out the morning
light. Of course, both the window and the house had
disappeared overnight.

Expectation or not, the sun was just rising as I awoke to the
smell and sound and splashes of a wet dog shaking herself dry.
Ah, wet dog. If you could bottle that scent, well, it could stay
bottled. Nobody would buy it.

Coming up from the creek was Maggie, my little Black Lab. I
could hear her giggle when she saw the drops of water her
shaking had left on my face and clothes.

"Hey, you should try the creek for a bath!" Her little girl
voice fit her compact body perfectly. "The water's not cold! I
think there's a hot spring or something."

I stared at her and then laughed. "We don't see each other for who knows how long and you want to talk about baths?"

"Well, it's either that or I'll go get wet and give you another shower!" She dropped her front legs into play stance and charged me.

We wrestled. Did I mention wet dog smell? By the time we were tired, she was dry, and I was sweating. It was a nice tired. I hadn't laughed, tickled, and been tickled so hard in a long time. Her cold wet nose knew just where to nuzzle to get me going: my ear, my neck, my nose.

"I've missed you, Maggie."

"I've missed you, too. It's been too long."

"Or, if it's like everything else I'm discovering up here, just long enough?"

"Maybe so," she said. "Maybe so." Her little girl voice didn't sound so little girl, now.

Pretty confident about how all this worked, I leaned back in the grass and asked her my question as she snuggled against me: "So what lesson are you going to give me?"

"Lesson? I'm your perpetual puppy. What could I teach you?"

I was perplexed. Each of the other dogs had been pretty clear about a lesson. Scout, reality; Trixie, loyalty; Snowboy, duty; and of course Suki, whose very name was love.

"Hmmm. No lesson? That doesn't make sense. Each dog has had a lesson for me, even if we had to work at them a little."

"Were these lessons different from your experiences with them before?" Again her little girl voice sounded wiser than the little girls I had known. At least the ones I had known before.

"No, I guess not. Maybe they weren't really lessons so much as reminders?" I thought about that. "They were just telling me what I already know."

"Know, but you may have forgotten, if that makes sense. Each of us dogs is just being who we are, you know?"

"Okay. So if I guess what you are most about, it's about how to play?"

"Yeah, that's probably true. You remember when I first went home with you? When Angelo was away?"

I remembered all too well what were among the darkest weeks of my life. "Oh yeah. I remember."

"Had you ever spent so much time on the floor? You laughed when I wrestled with the sticks—even when you were crying about Angelo. And tug of war—I think you were surprised at how strong a determined twelve-week-old puppy could be."

I smiled at the memory. She was right.

"So you came to teach me how to play?"

"I came—then and now—to remind you how, and how important it is, to play. Play is how we learn, how we create, how we heal."

"Wow, that's a pretty heavy definition."

"But you know it's true. Think about when your best ideas came to you. Was it while you were behind a desk? Or while walking or wrestling with a dog?"

"You know, for a dog, you're pretty smart."

"You know, for a human, you're not!" She tickled me till we both needed a nap.

It seemed to be early afternoon when I woke up, my arm wrapped around her, just like in the old days.

She opened one eye and smiled.

"Why do dogs do it? Why do you put up with us humans?"

"Well, you're funnier—and cheaper—than TV or the internet."

"No, I mean really. Even as puppies you seem wiser than most humans. Wiser, more fun, more loving."

"You humans fascinate us. You spend so much of your lives trying to unlearn what you know. Trying to forget what is in your genetic memory.

"Take play, again, for an example. We dogs didn't invent play. We just listened to that little voice inside us that says 'Go play.' Even when we get old, we listen to that voice.

"You humans, on the other paw—errr, hand—start telling your pups to get serious, work hard, and forget about play too early in their lives."

I twirled a blade of grass in my fingers as I considered this.

"See? Your hands like playing, even when you're not thinking about it. I think the only times you humans don't feel guilty about playing are when you're first in love, when you're alone with a dog, or when you see a *very* young child."

"Well, play is okay for kids, but honestly, life is pretty hard as an adult."

She sighed. "We've talked about this already, but sometimes it takes repetition for you humans to learn. So here we go: When did you work best or most creatively? When you were stressed out or when you were having fun?"

I thought back on my proudest accomplishments: The house I built, while I was full of laughter and awe. The books I'd written with a barely contained giggle always at the ready.

"See, the mistake you humans make is thinking that it's work *or* play. It's not an either/or thing. It's best when it's both!"

I reached over to rub the inside of her ears, something she'd always loved. Even though she was a dog, I could almost hear her purr.

"Okay," I admitted. "You win."

"I always do." She kissed me on the nose.

Time stretched out, like warm taffy in summer. At last I felt the need to ask my other question.

"So, I don't suppose you've seen Angelo."

Her eyes opened. "You know, a girl could get a complex. You got me from the shelter the last time he wasn't around. I tried to make you focus on sticks and rabbits and chase until he came back."

"You did! You did all of that until he came back and after!"

"Yeah, but once he was home, I knew…"

"Don't think that! I loved—love—you as much as I love him."

"Maybe, but you love him with the sparkle of your eyes, with the rhythm of your heart."

She paused, looked down at the grass, and I was, for once, silent.

"What the two of you have is special. A human gets to experience that kind of connection once or twice in a lifetime, if he's lucky. I'm not jealous, I guess, I'm just glad I get to remind both of you to play, that it's not all work, and to laugh."

"So he's here?"

"Not yet. The time isn't right. But soon."

She stood and walked away from me, toward the creek. When she returned she held not one, but two sticks in her mouth. She set them down on the ground in front of me as if they were precious china. I reached for one, and she met me with a growl.

"What the—"

"Not yet." She picked one of the sticks up and threw it into the creek. She grinned up at me and said one word: "Fetch!"

#######

Ssssweet childish thoughtsss of toyssss and thingssss. Thisss cutenesssss will neither ssstop nor sssslow the prosssecution.

7 FIDELITY

"Histories are more full of examples of the fidelity of dogs than of friends."
—Alexander Pope, English poet (1688-1744)

The mornings past had accustomed me to awaking in the company of one of my beloved canine friends. This morning, though, was different. I awoke by myself. No breakfast served, no tennis ball bouncing, no tinkling voice, no wet dog smell. Most of all, no Angelo. It was so silent that I wondered what happened even to the birds and crickets that might have filled the silence.

What I would have given for just one of Angelo's paws to slap me on the shoulder.

Walking along the ever-present creek, I saw that the trees were bare. The grass was brown but made no sound as I walked across it. It was eerie, this waking alone and the sounds of silence. I thought of the many morning walks I'd taken with the dogs in my life, watching the sun peek over the horizon, blushing in its innocence. I remembered the many times that Angelo's and my footprints were the first to be made in a new-fallen snow.

I missed that dog. Even seeing Scout, Trixie, Snowboy, Suki, and Maggie had not filled the void in my heart and in my arms. The melancholy silence of the morning only brought that emptiness into fullness. It had been with me since the morning I first awoke in this strange place.

The perpetually blue sky featured something different this morning: a few clouds gathered along what I think was the eastern horizon. The clouds' tops were the familiar fluffy white of cotton that Angelo and I had seen on our many walks together, but the bottoms were a dark and ominous grayish-black. Precisely the clouds that used to bring the lightning and thunder that so excited Angelo.

My emotions were as dark as the bottoms of those clouds. Out of curiosity, or maybe nostalgia, I began walking toward them. Only the sound of my own breathing gave any indication that I wasn't in a quiet vacuum. The sun rose far enough to light the tops of the clouds, giving them a golden halo.

Somewhere far in the distance I heard a rumble, a little like thunder, but I'd seen no lightning. I continued walking east. No, I wasn't imagining the rumble. At last. Sound, but still I didn't know what it was.

Then I heard a yelp. The sound was the running of dogs! Thousands of them! To the south of me, and to the north, I saw clouds of dust that reminded me of the stampedes in the many old western movies I'd watched as a kid.

I walked faster, and the rumbling grew louder. Cresting a ridge, I stopped hard. I gaped. I stood in awe.

From horizon to horizon, dogs. Everywhere. Proceeding like a well-orchestrated protest march. But there were no signs or banners. Just four-footed beings making their way forward. There were a very few two-footed creatures thrown in as well, although I didn't recognize any of them.

I jumped when I felt a hand on my shoulder and paws against my thigh. I turned around, and there were Cowboy, Trixie, Snowboy, Suki, and Maggie. They were all smiling, and looking pretty proud of themselves for finding me in this colossal crowd.

Cowboy's grin told me something good was happening, so I dared to ask, "What's going on?"

The dogs and Cowboy answered all at once, "Homecoming! Welcoming!" "Old One" "Never saw so many…" "…an honor, you know?"

"Whoa," I laughed. "Maybe just one of you can give me a clue?"

Suki took the lead, "It's a Grand Welcoming. It only happens once in a rare while. It's how we celebrate when one of the old souls return. Everyone talked about my return for weeks, but this is even more—"

"—magnificent," Trixie broke in. "I've never seen anything like it."

I looked at Cowboy.

"First time I've seen anything like it."

Snowboy looked like he was walking into a funeral, with only reverence and sobriety showing on his face. He probably didn't whisper in church, either.

Maggie nipped at my heels. "Come on, hurry! I wanna get closer!"

Our entourage began moving at a dignified trot.

As we made our way forward, the other celebrants parted to make way for us, as if they somehow knew that we needed to be at the forefront.

I glanced at the sky again, wondering if there were contingency plans to deal with rain. As well organized as this bunch was, I guessed that there were.

A crack of thunder split the air and everyone stopped. We found ourselves at the front of the crowd, which had shaped itself into a huge semicircle of humanity and caninity.

As the last echoes of the thunderclap died away, they were replaced by the opening strains of a spectacular fugue for a pipe organ.

"Bach, BWV552. You English speakers call it the St. Anne Fugue," I heard Snowboy whisper in my head, although all four of his feet were firmly planted on the ground. Telepathy, of course. The surprises never stopped coming.

The triumphant notes of music seemed to charm the clouds into parting. A light mist fell, creating a rainbow, perfect in its shape. The colors here seemed more vibrant than those I remembered from my previous life.

A dot appeared on the horizon, moving rocket-fast toward us. A black and white dot. As the shape approached us, it slowed to a canter and took on a familiar form.

Applause combined with the invisible pipe organ to shake the very ground we stood on. I knew that dot. That dog, that black and white rocket. My heart quickened. It was Angelo.

With both his regal tail and his intelligent head held high, the rainbow framed his body, and reflected in his eyes. Coming to a stop, his eyes swept the crowd, first from the left, a blink, then from the right, until they focused on me.

Somberly, he marched toward me, stood and placed his arms around my waist, his head pressed against my chest. My hand found that secret spot just below his right arm, and I hugged back. Through the tears in my eyes, the black and white of his fur were more beautiful than the colors of the rainbow in the sky. Black and white were the colors of the rainbow of my heart. The smell of sage was strong on him, as if he'd run through a field of it on his way to me.

The applause stopped, and one or two voices shouted "Beautiful!" through the light mist.

Angelo and I stood there, alone together in the midst of this crowd for a good long while. It felt like it was just the two of us. At last, he stood again on all four feet.

As orderly as the gathering had been, the dispersal was just as well orchestrated. Canine and human groups moved back in the direction from which we came. A few dozen canines came up to Angelo, sniffed him, and playfully put a paw on his back or licked his lips. "Congratulations" and "Welcome home" were not the only phrases I heard them say, but they were the most frequent.

At last, it was just our group. Somehow, either we had moved closer to the creek, or it had moved closer to us. After a week in this place, neither possibility would be worthy of surprise.

Angelo did a "down" on his own and looked like a sphinx with his front paws extended. The others followed suit and I found myself at the center of a circle.

Looking around that circle, I saw Angelo, Trixie, Snowboy, Suki, Maggie, and the only other two-legger, Cowboy. I was surrounded by five of my best canine and one of my best human friends. All at once, I realized that Scout wasn't with us.

"Hey, where's—"

"—Scout? He had other pressing duties to attend to," Snowboy offered.

"You know, this telepathy thing is a little scary," I returned, almost as a rebuke.

"We can talk about that later," Angelo commanded. "Right now, we've got some serious issues to deal with."

"Huh? Isn't this a place of no worries, land of milk and honey, and—"

"So you have been led to believe in your old life," Angelo interrupted. "The reality is, this is a place of laws and justice. And you seem to have been called to a trial."

"What?!" I sputtered.

Cowboy jumped in with military bluntness, "Is it serious?"

Angelo looked gravely at Cowboy and just as gravely at me. "We won't know for sure until we see the charges, but it doesn't look like it's going to be simple. They waited until we were all here to bring the case. For lesser charges, a human usually only needs one or two of his closest friends."

From above, an envelope dropped on the ground in front of me. It was heavy parchment. When I picked it up, I saw my name written in old-fashioned script. I turned it over, where I saw a heavy red wax seal, with a snake design pressed into it. I didn't want to open it.

Trixie's voice chimed, "Well. There's the summons. We'll deal with it. Together."

Angelo came to stand next to me.

"We'll deal with it together," I whispered into Angelo's ear.

"We'll deal with it together," he whispered back in his baritone voice. "We were and are and always will be there for each other. Fidelity. That's my word, that's my lesson. Fidelity."

My dog of few words had spoken.

#######

"SSSStepped on! Those cowsss nearly sssstepped on my sssublime tail! I will make complaintssssss," came the hissing voice from the limbs of a tree. But the ssssummonssss has been isssssssued at lassssst.

8 PREPARING

The best-laid schemes o' mice an' men
Gang aft agley,
An' lea'e us nought but grief an' pain,
For promis'd joy!
—Robert Burns, *To a Mouse*

At Angelo's suggestion, Cowboy would stay behind until the trial began. I waved good-bye to him as we began our journey, single file, into town. First we walked on a dusty road and then on a cobblestone street. Eventually we crossed the ubiquitous creek on an old timber bridge. Beyond an expansive lawn lay a simple adobe building with "Courthouse" in raised letters, black on white. My compatriots paused with anticipation as I turned the doorknob.

Angelo put his paw on my leg, looked up at me, and whispered, "I'm with you. We're all with you."

I returned his look, hesitated, realizing I didn't even know what we were doing, and then replied, "I know."

45

I held the door open for my entourage, watching first Trixie, then Snowboy, Suki, Maggie, and Angelo walk ahead of me, tails held proud and high. Proud of what, I wondered. Of me?

Trixie checked us in with the receptionist, who had to be at least part Rottweiler. Her contempt for me came through loud and clear with a growled, "*He* will have to wait there, on the human bench. Try to keep him quiet." Her big eyes looked over my friends, clearly questioning their choice of companions.

"I'll call the Public Defender's Office. Sit!" The receptionist made no move toward a telephone or anything else. She returned to her magazine, sniffing the print as her eyes regained their empty stare. Suddenly, she let out a howl, followed by a bark. Moments later, in the distance, I could hear an answering baritone howl. Angelo leaned into my ear and translated, "He'll be here shortly."

So, we waited. I fidgeted. The dogs whispered among themselves. The receptionist gave a disapproving growl in our direction every now and again. Finally, the door opened, and a German Shepherd walked in like he owned the place. He sniffed the corners of the room before sparing any attention for us.

Clearly well versed in canine hierarchy, he first greeted Angelo, our little pack's alpha, and moved down the line.

I was, of course, the last to be greeted. He sat on his haunches and thrust out his paw. "Hayes. And you are…"

Right. Like there were hundreds of humans he could mistake me for. "I'm Leland." Surnames seemed to be superfluous in this place.

"Well, we have a lot of preparation to do and not a lot of time. Let's see if we can find somewhere to talk." He swaggered to the receptionist's desk and, unintimidated by her ferocity, flirted with her ear. She nearly purred. When he turned back toward us, he had a fox-guarding-the-henhouse grin on his face.

"Let's go." With that, we advanced through the other door of the room into a long hall, punctuated with doorways short and tall. I gazed at some of the paintings on the wall. Various breeds of canines were depicted, but all wore judicial robes. Whenever I slowed down to appreciate them, Suki nipped at my heels, clearly warning me to hurry up.

At last we came to a room with a dilapidated conference table, and enough raggedy chairs for our group to sit on. Clearly the lush rooms we had walked past were for more worthy miscreants.

We entered the room, with Hayes choosing a chair at the head of the table, my friends along the far side of the table, and me with my back to the door.

"Right. I assume you know how these things work?" Without even acknowledging my blank look, he continued, "Of course not." His manner, while not disrespectful, was dismissive.

I looked at my canine compatriots across the conference room table, and I saw the definition of boredom. Trixie's head lay on the table, with a small pool of drool beginning to form. Snowboy stared into space in a Zen-like trance. Suki's eyes were rolled back in her head as she lay back in her reclining chair. Maggie was batting a ballpoint pen from one paw to the other. Only Angelo was watching my face, as if to make sure I understood what was being said. Even his eyelids looked heavy. Apparently canine civics classes were more complete than their human counterparts.

Hayes continued his monologue, as if he had recited it thousands of times before. Perhaps he had. "The prosecution will open the case, presenting a summary of..."

I awoke from my lethargy. "Prosecution?"

"Yes, the prosecution. That's just another name for the lawyer representing the larger pack..."

"I understand that, but what am I accused of?"

I saw the word "pitiful" pass through his mind from one eye to the other. "Yes, well, we'll get to that. Now, where was I? Oh yes, the prosecution will open, telling the judge and everyone what you are accused of, briefly mentioning the evidence, and then it's the defense's—that's us—turn to present an overview of why you are blameless and innocent. Are you with me so far?"

I nodded absent-mindedly. What could I possibly be accused of? Then again, there were so many things that I *could* be accused of.

Hayes had continued without my attention, "...their witnesses, and then we get to cross-examine them, poking holes in their testimony wherever we can. The prosecution can then redirect examination of the witnesses, attempting to patch the holes we've found. Then it's our turn to call witnesses who support our case, if we have any. The defense will cross-examine them, and I'll redirect examination of them. After that, the prosecutor will summarize their case, then I summarize your innocence, and then it's in the paws of the jury."

Again, my head nodded, as if it were on autopilot.

"I've studied a little about you humans and your justice system. You will notice some differences. Our juries are of variable numbers. Yours will have five. And we don't waste a lot of time qualifying and disqualifying jury members. We rely on the inherent honesty and fairness of the canine mind and heart."

I glanced across the table. Where there was boredom before, there was now a symphony of snores. Not even Angelo had succeeded in keeping his eyes open.

Hayes proceeded to ask me a great many questions that, in my mind, had no bearing on a potential criminal case, but he was the lawyer, so I acquiesced.

Mother's name? Yes. Littermates/Siblings? Yes. Urinary tract infections? No. Eat broccoli? No. Fixed or intact? Intact. Ouch! And on and on. He recorded all the answers on a yellow legal pad. At least some things were consistent across cultures, although this tablet was writing the words by itself. "Is there anything else you think I should know as I prepare your defense?"

I was boggled. I had no idea of the crime, nor a firm grip on how the system worked, and yet he was asking me for help with the defense? Not a good sign. "Well, let me think," I stalled. "What again, exactly, am I charged with?"

Hayes looked at me coldly. "This isn't about one act or one alleged crime. This is about your life: how you lived it, what you did with it, who you shared it with. It's about whether you deserve to be a member of the pack."

"I've always loved dogs, and dogs have always loved me!" I practically shouted.

"I guess I've won cases with less than that."

Somewhere, a very large bell tolled.

Hayes addressed me. "Well, it's time. Let's go to court."

9 JUSTICE

A dog is better than I am, for he has love and does not judge.
—Abba Xanthias, monk of the Desert Fathers

"All rise for the Honorable Judge Scout!" the bailiff, a Dalmatian, cried out. What the... Then a door to the judge's chambers opened, and there was Scout, in a black robe. Power of imagination? Who the heck imagined this?

The bailiff continued, "Case number 66529, The Pack vs. Human Leland."

The judge—I was still having a hard time believing it was Scout—intoned, "Sit! Stay!" The whole room did exactly that. All sniffing, barking, and whispering stopped instantaneously. I was glad to see that Cowboy was in the gallery.

The jury box was empty. From the times I had served on human juries, this struck me as unusual. And where was the prosecutor? I looked at the table to the left. Vacant, I thought as I noted a single file folder on the prosecutor's table. A moment later I realized how wrong I was. The chair was occupied by an unusual body. Two unblinking eyes met mine. A forked tongue sampled the air. I closed my eyes. This had to be a dream—no, a nightmare.

Trixie's paw touched my shoulder, reassuring me.

Judge Scout spoke, "Are the prosecuting and defending attorneys prepared to try this case?"

Hayes rose, "Yes, your honor."

The prosecutor rose to his full height—length? "Yessss, your honor."

Judge Scout continued, "Very well. Please state your full names, for the record."

This time, the prosecutor started, "Nicholas Beales, Esq., your Honor. Bub, to my friends."

Friends? This reptile had friends?

"Hayes, Rex Hayes, your honor," my attorney stated.

"And is the defendant present?"

Hayes nudged me, and I stood. "Yes, your honor."

Scout—Judge Scout—gave me an appraising stare. Somewhere off in the distance I heard a gurgle of water, maybe the creek, through the open windows of the courtroom.

"Very well. Let's begin. Would the bailiff please read the charges?"

The Dalmatian recited from memory: "Disloyalty, dereliction of duty, failure to love with abandon, unplayful behavior, and lack of fidelity."

"Does the defendant understand the charges being brought against him?" intoned the Shorthaired Pointer I had thought was a friend.

Hayes sat up straight and said, "Yes, your Honor, he does."

I stared at Hayes with disbelief. "I do?" I felt Suki nip at my heels and I repeated, "I do," without the question mark. Ouch!

His eyebrows arched, Scout, his *honor* Scout, pounded his gavel. "Very well, let's get this show on the road."

"Would the prosecutor care to make an opening statement?"

"Yesssss, your honor, I ssshould like that very much...."
Prosecuting counsel Beales slid off his chair toward the podium,

wrapped himself around it, and wound his way to the top. He coiled there, almost as if he were preparing to strike.

"Over thessse lassst ssseveral dayssss, I have ssssseen the defendant exhibit unsssseemly behavior with hissss compadresssss from hisss previoussss life. Hypocrissssssy perssssssonified—"

"Your honor, I object," Hayes rose to attention "May we ask the prosecutor to refrain from hissss, errr, his theatrical lisp? It's giving this attorney and his client a splitting headache."

His honor Scout considered this and ruled, "Prosecutor will refrain from hissing unless absolutely necessss, errr, necessary."

"I shall attempt to comply, your honor, with prejudissss, but with respect for my essssst, errr, esteemed colleague."

"Now, where was I?" Even without the theatrics, Mr. Beales had just a trace of a lisp. Eyeing the courtroom gallery, he continued, "Oh, yes. Over these last several days, I have seen the defendant exhibit unseemly behavior with his compadres from his previous life. Even as they reminded him of the lessons they had attempted to teach him in that life, he had nothing but callous disregard for them."

"Today, I will offer convincing evidence why this—thisss human—should be denied entrance to this sacred place and refused membership in the pack."

Just like watching Perry Mason reruns on TV. Well, except for the fact that the prosecutor was a snake, and the judge and my attorney were both dogs. Maybe it was more like Animal Planet presents Judge Judy. Oh yeah, and the jury box was still empty.

"Would the defense attorney care to make his opening statement?"

The prosecutor twined his way down and back to his table. Hayes stood and placed his forepaws on the podium. His German Shepherd eyes, brown as berries, spoke his sincerity even before his voice did. He allowed those eyes to wander over the assemblage silently.

Judge Scout's impatient voice interrupted the moment, "Well, speak!"

"Canines and honorary canines, Mr. Beales has assured you that he has evidence of my client's unworthiness. I, like you, am eager to see this alleged evidence. Though I have not known my client long—"

Yeah, about an hour, I thought, but he knows more about my pedigree and health than my own mother.

"—he has impeccable credentials. His character references," here he waved a paw at my five canine and one token human friends, "speak highly and lovingly of him. We will show today that not only is he worthy of entrance, but that he would be an excellent example of caninity for other pack members to emulate."

"I ask you to keep an open mind and an open heart, as we refute and prove groundless the prosecutor's allegations. Thank you." With that, his forepaws hit the ground and he sauntered back to the defense table with his tail held high.

The young Beagle court stenographer watched his swagger, almost swooning. I suppose her adoration wouldn't really have an effect on the accuracy of the reporting. She was using one of those magic self-writing tablets that Suki had used days earlier. The stenographer licked her chops to keep the drool from leaving her lips.

His honor pounded his gavel and spoke, "We'll take a short recess—a potty break—and then we'll begin taking witness testimony. Please clean up after yourselves and help those who cannot clean up for themselves."

The bailiff opened the courtroom door and all the dogs walked outside, using the spacious courtyard lawn for their sanitary needs.

Hayes turned to me, still in the courtroom, and whispered, "I think that went well."

I assumed he had lost his mind. "Went well? I don't even know what I'm supposed to have done! Or what the punishment is!"

"You told the judge you understood the charges," he admonished. "Let's not have perjury added to your problems."

"What's with the snake?"

"Nicholas? Oh, he got in on a law-and-order ticket in the last election. Really a nice fellow. Just doing his job. Still makes me uncomfortable, though, that he can't shake hands."

The door at the back of the courtroom opened again. A parade of dogs, led by Judge Scout, entered and took their seats in a most quiet and efficient manner.

"Now, keep your mouth shut and just act as respectful and intelligent as you can," Hayes coached me in one last whisper.

"All rise!" shouted the bailiff. "This court is now in session!"

Judge Scout poured himself a bowl of water and we were ready to begin.

TRIXIE'S TESTIMONY

Nicholas Beales, the prosecuting attorney, slithered to the base of, and then to the top of, the podium. "We call Miss Trixie, the English Shepherd, to testify."

There was a gasp in the courtroom, and I realized a moment later that it was my gasp. No one else seemed surprised. Judge Scout frowned at me, and so did Hayes.

Trixie loped from the gallery to the witness stand, beside but at a lower level than the judge's bench.

The bailiff swore her in. I tried but couldn't see what book she placed her paw on. I made a mental note to ask her later, assuming I'd ever get to talk to her again.

"Pleasssse—sorry your honor—please state your name and breed for the record."

"Trixie, English Shepherd."

"And how did you come to know the defendant?"

"I was with his family from before the time he was born."

"So you were the first dog he knew?"

Trixie was beaming with pride. "The very first. We played together. I pulled him in his little red—"

"Yes, yessss, we'll have time for all of that later. Please just answer the questions. What was the character trait that you were to teach the defendant? The lesson you were to teach him, indeed his whole family?"

Now Trixie looked nervously first at the prosecutor, then at the judge, and finally at me. She spoke quietly, "Loyalty."

"Do you think you were a good teacher?"

Again she answered quietly, "I do."

"Please explain for the court a few of the ways you attempted to teach the humans…" Here my doubt that snakes had facial expressions dissipated as Mr. Beales, Esq., was clearly sneering. "…the noble quality of loyalty."

Trixie thought for a moment. "Wherever the boy walked, I was at his side. When he wandered too far, I nudged him toward home. Each night, when the family went in the house to sleep, I slept at their door so that no intruder could pass without my knowledge."

"Outside? The humans made you sleep outside?"

Hayes rose. "Objection, your honor. The defendant was a pup, errr, child. He had no control of—"

Beales interrupted, "It's not an issue of control. I'm trying to determine if the defendant had any concern for a loyal friend being left outdoors in an extreme climate."

Judge Scout stated his decision: "Overruled. Miss Trixie, please answer the question." Hayes sat down.

Her voice quavered, "I don't remember the question."

Beales nearly bellowed the question again, "Did the humans make you sleep outdoors in the cold, snow, sleet, and rain? Like some kind of wild animal?"

"I slept outdoors, as much by my choice as theirs."

"Yes or no, please." Beales glared at Trixie.

Meekly, she answered, "Yes."

"And when you were sick, did they take you to a doctor?"

"That wasn't their—"

"Yes or no, please."

She whispered, "No."

"And when it became apparent that you were not going to recover from distemper? What did they do to ease your pain?"

Looking intently at the floor, Trixie mumbled.

"I'm sorry, I couldn't hear you."

"The father put me down," she was still barely audible.

"You mean they killed you?"

"Yes! The boy's mother couldn't stand seeing me suffer, so his father—"

"His father did what?"

"Objection, your honor! This has nothing to do with the defendant. Relevance?" I was starting to think that Hayes was earning his pay. If he was being paid.

"Again, your honor, I'm establishing whether the human," Beales practically spat the word out, "had any compassion, any loyalty to his faithful canine companion."

The judge hesitated for only a second. "Objection sustained. You've had ample opportunity to establish the defendant's reactions and feelings. Do you have any more questions for Miss Trixie?"

"No further questions, your honor." Pouting did not look good on a serpent.

"Your witness, Hayes." Beales slithered back to his table.

Hayes stood and walked toward the witness. He put his paw on the low wall of the witness stand.

He began, "Were you happy living with the humans? Your humans?"

The sparkle returned to Trixie's eyes and her voice. "Oh, yes! We had so much fun. They loved me, and I loved them so much."

Hayes looked comfortable leaning against the witness box. His calm demeanor obviously put Trixie at ease. "What is your happiest memory from that time?"

"Every summer, the boy—the defendant, I mean—and his brothers would set up a pup tent in a field of dandelions. We'd chase the dandelion seeds as they floated on the air. We'd watch the clouds together, lying next to each other. At night, we counted the stars. It was wonderful!"

"Did you sleep with them in the tent?"

"No. You see, I really don't like enclosed spaces. They make me feel as if I have to escape."

"So you slept outside. Would you say that you *chose* to sleep outside?"

"Yes, yes, I would. The boy—the defendant—tried to get me to sleep in the tent with them, but I wouldn't go in. I'm ashamed to say I even growled at him when he got a little bit forceful."

"Overall, would you say the human family was good to you?"

"I couldn't have asked for any better. One time, when the family went on vacation, they didn't tell the boy that I wasn't going along until just as they were leaving. He jumped out of the car and said if I wasn't going then he wasn't either. Little guy put up quite a fight. And before you ask—" she eyed the prosecutor "—they did not leave me unattended. The boy's uncle stayed with me."

"That sounds like he was pretty loyal."

"He was—is—fiercely loyal!"

"Thank you, Miss Trixie, for your testimony."

Turning to the judge, Hayes said, "No further questions, your honor."

The judge eyed Beales and asked, "Redirect?"

"Yesssss. We certainly will." Staying at the prosecutor's table, he faced Trixie and asked, "When you were dying—"

"Objection your honor! We've established that this line of questioning—"

"Sustained. If that's the only question you have, Mr. Beales, I believe we can let Miss Trixie step down."

Mr. Beales' tail rattled in anger. Judge Scout scowled at him. The tail silenced.

As Trixie stepped from the witness stand, she turned toward the jury box. I thought maybe she was confused from the stress of testifying, but she walked purposefully to the jury box and sat down. I wished I could ask Hayes what that was all about. Trixie's eyes met mine and were still sparkling.

SNOWBALL'S TESTIMONY

Meanwhile, back at the judge's bench, Judge Scout asked, "Mr. Beales, is your next witness ready?"

"Yesss, your honor. The prosecution calls Snowball, the Chow-Pomeranian mix, alias Snowboy."

So, it appeared that all my dogs would be called. I had no idea whether that was good news or bad.

Snowboy somberly walked to the stand and, without prompting, recited the witness' oath.

Mr. Beales began the questioning from his table. "Please share with us how you came to know the defendant."

"I lived with him and his family."

"Yesss, yes, but how did you come to live with them?" Beales' tail rattled once in annoyance. It was almost fun seeing Beales getting annoyed.

"When my previous family moved, they relocated me to be with the boy's family."

"Relocated? Don't you mean 'gave' you to them?"

"A being of free will goes where he chooses."

"So you chose to live with this family?"

"I chose to do my duty, and my duty called for me to be with this family." Now it was Snowboy's turn to growl in annoyance.

"Ah, yes, duty. That was your specialty, wasn't it?"

"Was and is."

"Can you humor the court with your definition of duty?"

As if speaking to the village idiot, Snowboy complied. "Duty is doing the right thing, at the right time, for the right reasons, without regard to the cost to one's self."

"In your time with this family of humans, did you strive to teach them about duty?"

"I did."

"Do you think you were successful?"

"That, sir, is not for me to judge."

"Very well. Let's examine some facts, then." Beales appeared for all the world to be pacing back and forth in front of Snowboy, but snakes can't pace, can they?

"When you first arrived with this family, did the boy speak to you?"

"Not for some time."

"What were his first words to you?"

"I believe he asked me to be quiet."

"Mr. Snowball, may I remind you that you are under oath?"

"Yes, sir, you may." This smart-aleckiness was something I'd never seen before in Snowboy. I liked it.

At the prosecutor's table, Beales looked at his tablet—another magic tablet; clever device—"Could his first words have been 'Shut up'?"

Beales, that snake in the grass, had been eavesdropping when Snowboy and I were talking!

"I don't recall his exact words."

"What was the license plate number of the family's car?"

"78-B233."

"When was the boy's birthday?"

"January—"

"Objection, your honor!" Hayes howled the words out, "Is counsel going to subject us to a piece-by-piece biography of the defendant?"

"Your honor, I'm merely trying to establish that Mr. Snowball has an uncanny memory for details and that it's highly unlikely that he cannot recall—"

"Silence!" Judge Scout's voice rivaled thunder in its volume and intensity. "Would the prosecutor have us believe that he is calling the esteemed Mr. Snowboy—who is, if I may remind Mr. Beales, a witness called by the prosecution—a liar?"

Beales seethed. "No, your honor, I would never question Mr. Ssssnowball's integrity."

"Good. Objection is sustained. And please try not to antagonize your own witness!"

Mr. Beales took a moment to control his anger and to decide on his next line of questioning.

Turning again to Snowboy, he continued, "You died trying to save this boy, didn't you?"

"Yes. It was my duty. I swore to keep him safe."

"Did he try to save you? To do the right thing by you?"

"He was too young to try to save me, but he did do the right thing."

"And that was?"

"He stayed with me. He held me as I died. He set me free."

"But he did nothing to save you?"

"My physical body was beyond saving. He set my spirit free and that was fulfillment of his duty. Above and beyond, I'd say."

Knowing he was beaten, Beales addressed Judge Scout, "Your honor, no further questions."

Judge Scout, scarcely suppressing a snicker, said, "I'd have guessed not. Defense?"

"Your honor, I believe Mr. Snowball's testimony is complete. We thank him."

"Yes, yes, as well you should." Losing the battle with a stifled chuckle, Judge Scout declared, "We're taking a ten-minute recess. Remember to clean up…" And his chuckle grew into a guffaw.

Outdoors, I tried not to watch as Hayes took care of his business. When I heard the crinkle of a poop bag, I figured it was safe to start a conversation. "So what kind of law school do you go to to prepare to be a public defender?"

"Practicing canine law takes much less schooling than human law. We German Shepherds have an innate sense of logic that helps a lot. In my previous life, I lived with one of your human lawyers. I picked up some of the finer points of law from watching Court TV with him."

"Court TV? But what university?"

"Oh, look at the time! We need to get back in there."

Hayes bumped into the Beagle court stenographer. They walked in together.

I walked in with only my thoughts as company. Lived with a lawyer? Watched TV?

SUKI'S TESTIMONY

"The prosecution calls Miss Suki, the Shiba Inu, to testify." Beales' hiss was barely noticeable this time, despite all the S sounds.

Suki pranced, with her tail in its perpetual question mark, to the witness stand. Her almond-shaped eyes were bright with anticipation. After the bailiff swore her in, she hopped up into the chair.

Beales crawled to the witness stand and stretched up to hold Suki in his hypnotic gaze. "Please tell the court how you came to know the defendant." Beales swayed back and forth. He wasn't trying to—no, surely even he wouldn't—hypnotize her? The sparkle in her eyes grew just a little dimmer with each of Beales' sways.

Her voice, less sing-songy than usual, was slow. "He... adopted me when I was seven and a half weeks old."

"How old would you say he was when he adopted you?" Back and forth his head moved.

"Forty-two years, I think."

"Forty-two? That's much older than I would have thought. Why do you think he adopted you more than 30 years after Mr. Snowball left his life?"

"He said he needed love, that all the love had died in his life."

"And he expected you, a seven-and-a-half-week-old puppy, to replace all that love, from all those years?"

"He was happy to have crumbs, didn't need the whole cake he said."

I teared up, remembering when I told her that, the first night she was in my house and in my life. Did Hayes realize she was being hypnotized? A glance at him told me that he was falling into a trance, too. And so was Judge Scout. That sneaky snake. What could I do?

"Was he a good parent to you?"

"Wouldn't let me sleep with him first night. Kennel, like a den, he said..." She was all but nodding off.

I stood up, tipping my chair over so that it crashed to the ancient wooden floor, "Objection!"

Hayes shook his head and looked at me with shock. The judge, too, was released from the trance, and automatically shouted, "Order! What is your objection?"

"Your honor, the prosecutor was, he was, well, it looked like he was hypnotizing you all."

"Ridiculous!" shouted Beales. "Such a thing would be unconscionable."

Hayes asked me in a whisper, "Are you sure?"

"Yes, I'm sure!"

"This is a serious charge, Mr. Beales. You have been accused—for the second time in this court in as many months—of serious misconduct. After the trial, we'll be discussing these allegations. In *depth*, we'll be discussing them. Do I have your word of honor that you will refrain from this sort of thing?"

I almost felt sorry for Beales. He looked so forlorn, so remorseful, and yet so guilty! "Yes, your honor."

"Very well. You may continue questioning Miss Suki. I believe she was about to tell you how she came to know the defendant. Stenographer, can you read back the last couple of sentences of testimony from the tablet?"

The Beagle stenographer—and the judge's—eyes grew wide when she read entire paragraphs back that none but I and the magic tablet remembered.

"Perhaps, Mr. Beales, there will be less alleging and more punishing. Now, continue."

"So, Miss Suki, your previous testimony confirmed that the defendant had been without a canine companion for over thirty years. Did that seem odd to you?"

"No, sir, the defendant had spent a large part of that time traveling. He got me when his life 'settled down,' he said."

"And you believed him?"

"I did and I do."

"So he spent all of his time with you?"

"As much as he could. He had to do something he called 'work' a lot."

"Tell us about your name. It's Japanese, isn't it?"

"Yes, my ancestors came from Japan. My breed is one of the oldest known to mankind. We originated—"

"Yes, yes, all very nice, but your name. What does it mean?

"Oh. It means 'love.'"

"Love. Such a nice sounding word. Do you think the human mind can comprehend its meaning?"

Suki waited a moment before she answered, "I do. We show them unlimited love every day we share their lives, and if they don't learn, well, we just have to try harder."

Beales twirled around to face the dogs in the gallery. "Was it love that you felt when he caged you when he went to this place called 'work'?"

"It was a kennel, not a cage. He didn't want me to hurt myself while he was away."

"Isn't it possible he caged you so that you wouldn't damage his precious 'things'?"

"I don't think so. No, I don't believe that for a minute."

How did Beales do that? How did he look like he was pacing?

"Did he always cage you?"

"No. As I got older, he often let me have the run of the house, even when he was gone."

"On September 9, 2003—" Beales was referring to his magic tablet "—did he let you have the run of the house, as you put it?"

"I've never been very good with calendars…"

"I have here a sworn affidavit from the poodle that lived next door to you in Denver. He swears to that fact."

"Well, then, it must be true."

"He also swears that he saw you running up and down the stairs of your house with something white in your mouth. Does that refresh your memory?"

Suki blushed and uttered, "Oh."

"Please tell the court what you recall now."

"Well, that must have been the day—"

"Yes?"

"The day I unrolled a whole roll of toilet paper and carried it all over the house. All in one piece!" She was done blushing and was beaming with pride. Maggie applauded from the gallery.

Judge Scout pounded his gavel. "Silence!"

"And what was the defendant's reaction when he saw this?"

"He was furious—at first—and then we laughed together."

Obviously not the answer Beales wanted. He continued, "And he caged you again after that?"

"No. But he did keep the bathroom doors closed."

"He *never* caged you again?"

"Maybe once or twice, like when he'd take me to the doctor."

"Did you get to leave the house often?"

"Oh, yes! We'd go for walks two or three times a day! And to the dog park, and then we got a big kennel on wheels and visited forty-six states. Whatever states are."

Beales saw this witness sliding away from him and decided to cut his losses. "No further questions, your honor," he abruptly addressed Judge Scout.

"Cross-examine, Mr. Hayes?"

Hayes smirked and said, "Yes, please." He walked in front of the witness stand. "So you travelled with the defendant a lot?"

"It was so exciting! We saw both oceans—the deserts—the mountains—and so many of his friends!"

"The defendant had a lot of friends?"

"Oh, yes. And so many of them had dogs I could talk and play with."

"Were you with him still when the war started?"

She cast her eyes down. "Yes. Yes, I was."

"You seem sad about that. Why?"

"Wars are sad. People killing people is always sad. But it broke my heart to see him cry when he watched the news."

"Did the defendant do anything unusual during the war?"

"Unusual? Well, I don't know if it's unusual—I suppose it is…. He started sending packages. Lots of packages. Right after his friend Cowboy was sent to Iraq."

"Packages? What did he put in them?"

"Sometimes cookies, toothpaste, soap, books, a lot of stuff. After a while, he was sending parcels to a dozen or more people at a time. He didn't even know some of them."

"And?"

"And he'd always stop in front of Cowboy's package, like he was praying, before he put stuff in it."

"Why did he do that?"

"I think he loved—loves—Cowboy."

Oh how I wished she hadn't brought all this up. Now my eyes teared up.

"Did you do anything to encourage this love?"

"I did. I always dropped one of my tennis balls in the package for Cowboy."

Judge Scout dabbed at one eye.

"That's beautiful. One more question. One I think Mr. Beales meant to ask." Hayes smirked at the prosecutor. "What was your lesson for the defendant, and do you think you were successful in teaching it?"

"My name was my lesson: Love. And yes, I was successful. Very successful." Her eyes went back and forth between Cowboy and me.

"No further questions, your honor."

"Redirect, Mr. Beales?"

"Certainly not!"

I believe Mr. Beales was beside himself. I think snakes can do that.

"You may step down, Miss Suki," Judge Scout offered. She, too, went to the jury box, where she nuzzled Trixie.

ANGELO'S TESTIMONY

"The prosecution calls Mr. Angelo, the Border Collie."

Angelo arose from his seat in the gallery, raised his proud tail and raced to the witness stand. The bailiff was unsuccessful in trying to hide his reverence when he administered the witness' oath.

Mr. Beales stayed at the prosecutor's table to ask his questions. I wondered if he'd heard about Angelo's victory over a certain rattlesnake in the wilds of Colorado some years ago.

"Please state your name, sir." Wow. Beales was actually showing some respect. This was new.

"Angelo, the Border Collie."

"And how did you come to know the defendant?"

Angelo's eyes were on me, not the prosecutor.

"I found him. He needed me."

"Perhaps you'd be kind enough to share a few details?" I thought at first that Beales was being sarcastic, but I realized this too was his way of showing respect.

"When Miss Suki was killed by a hit-and-run driver, I *happened* to be in the area."

"Happened?"

"I was sent," his eyes glanced upward, "and requested," his eyes shifted to Suki, "to be in the area. To keep an eye on the defendant."

"A sort of surveillance?"

"Oh, no, more a kind of guardianship. The defendant is well-loved."

Beales glowered. Clearly he didn't like the direction this testimony was going, so he changed tactics.

"Your lesson for the defendant was—"

"Fidelity. Faithfulness. To always be there for someone else. Someone you love."

"Did he learn it?"

"Yes." Laconic. Border Collies always were.

"On March 1, 2010, where were you?"

Unlike Suki, Angelo apparently had no problems with calendars.

"Walking. Walking with the Man through the snow in Colorado."

"And at the end of that walk, were you still with the defendant?"

Angelo's chin jutted out. "No."

"Where were you?"

"I was—distracted. I chased something and I—got lost."

"Got lost?" Beales peered at Angelo's prominent nose. "With a fine olfactory organ such as that, you got lost?"

"It was that organ—and another, lower down—that caused me distraction. And when the, um, distraction was complete, I was a long way from the Man.

"Surely the defendant was looking for you? Shouting your name, following your paw prints? Being there for someone he loved?"

"I've heard that he searched."

"Heard?"

"I didn't see it myself, I—"

Beales cut him off with "No further questions, your honor."

Angelo looked frustrated. He was used to leading, not being led. And I didn't understand what Beales was trying to do.

"Judge Scout looked at Beales disapprovingly. "Mr. Hayes, cross-examine?"

"Yes, sir."

"Mr. Angelo. I believe you were going to tell us why you didn't see the man searching—"

"Objection!" Beales shouted. "The witness' reason is irrelevant to this case."

"Your honor, I think it's quite relevant, though surely every canine and maybe every human in this room knows the story." Hayes was reaching for the book that each witness had touched while being sworn in.

"Hold it right there, Mr. Hayes. In this case, I believe the prosecutor's objection is valid. We're establishing the fidelity of the defendant, not the witness." The look of surprise on Hayes' face was mirrored, I'm sure, by my own. This was the first time the judge had ruled in Beales' favor.

"Very well, then. Mr. Angelo, can you think of any way that the defendant was faithful to you—ways in which he showed fidelity?"

Angelo hesitated, and then answered confidently, "Every single day that we've been together, we start the day with a walk. Every day. I awake him with my paw on his shoulder, he groans, and then he gets up and we go. We watch the sunrises together. I chase a rabbit and he waits for me. He moves slower than I do—what human doesn't?—so sometimes I wait for him. Then he works, and I watch. He puts treats in with my food. He rubs that place above my tail where I can never reach. He loves me. Every day. Every day, he's there for me. That's fidelity, and he's got it."

The courtroom was silent, and it looked blurry through my tears. Border Collies, I guess, aren't always laconic.

"Thank you, Mr. Angelo," Hayes said, taking a white handkerchief from his, well, from somewhere.

Judge Scout looked Mr. Beales in the eye and asked, "Redirect?"

Beales appeared to be weighing his options. "Yes, your honor. Just a couple more questions."

"Go ahead, then."

"Mr. Angelo, were you intact—you know what I mean—when you met the defendant?"

Angelo blushed and gave his one-word answer: "Yes."

"Did the defendant ever talk about neutering you?"

Hayes was slow in his objection, distracted by the stenographer's batting eyelashes. He objected one second after Angelo said, "Yes."

Below the belt, and sure to influence every male in the courtroom.

Hayes asked one more question: "And what was your response."

With a flush of shame coloring the white of his muzzle, Angelo answered, "I bit him."

"No further questions, your honor."

Angelo walked to the jury box, his tail dragging on the floor.

MAGGIE'S TESTIMONY

"The pack calls Maggie Galong, the Black Labrador."

Maggie ran up to the witness box. The bailiff offered the witness' oath, and her response was "Yeah, yeah, yeah."

Before Beales could even open his mouth, Maggie blurted out, "Look, I've listened to you ask everybody the same questions, or almost the same, so here are my answers. He got me at a shelter, I taught him how to play again, he cried a lot when he first got me, and yeah, he learned how to play really well."

Sputtering, Beales lectured her, "Young lady, I'll thank you to answer the questions that I put to you, and no others. Now, please tell the court how you came to know him?"

It's amazing how far a Black Labrador's eyes can roll back in her head. "He. Got. Me. At. A. Shelter. Didja catch it that time?"

The red started at the end of Beales' tail and worked its way up his body like a thermometer. "Young lady, no sarcasm please." He looked at Judge Scout for help, but Judge Scout's paw was obscuring a big smile.

"Why do you think he got you from a shelter?"

"He was lonesome. He missed his buddy Angelo. He was going nuts and hadn't laughed forever. And because I was the cutest dog at the shelter. He was a soft touch. I just walked up to the fence and started licking his hand. He knew he wanted me."

"Miss Maggie, please, just answer the questions I ask."

"I did!"

"Do you think he got you as a replacement for Angelo?"

"I have no idea. If he did, that would have been stupid. I'm not a Border Collie, in case you didn't notice. I run fast, but not that fast, and I have NO interest in herding. None. Zero. Zilch."

"Did he treat you well?"

"Like a princess. There were treats, and tennis balls, and toys, and books to chew on. But he asked me not to chew on the books, so I stopped. Still, every now and again I get this craving for Elizabeth Barrett Browning. Very tasty."

The angry red on Beale's body had reached to about the 150-degree mark.

"So how did you teach him to play?" Can snakes clench their teeth?

"Like this!" From nowhere, Maggie found a tennis ball—imagined it?—picked it up with her mouth and threw it to me. I caught it, and threw it back as I had done a thousand times. But this time, there was a snake's head between us. Oops. The ball hit Nicholas Beales right in the kisser. This was probably not good.

Judge Scout's paw came away from his face, and where there had been a smile, there was now incredulity. "Order! Order!" as he pounded his gavel so hard I thought his bench would crack.

In that moment of silence, Maggie answered one unasked question: "I think I was very successful in teaching him how to play." She giggled.

"We'll take a brief recess and hope the prosecutor recovers."

There was definitely murmuring as the crowd moved outdoors for the recess. Maggie came out and a couple of other Black Lab pups high-fived her. She was still giggling. Apparently none of the witnesses were allowed to talk to me, so it was just Hayes and me.

He was furious. "Of all the stupid, idiotic, numbskull things I have seen in the courtroom, that was the worst. You'd best say a prayer that our friend Nicholas Beales wasn't injured by that tomfoolery. What were you thinking?"

"I wasn't thinking. It was instinct. Maggie and I have played fetch with a tennis ball practically since the first day I got her! My body just reacted when the tennis ball came into my hand!"

"Judge Scout does not take kindly to such buffoonery in his courtroom."

Sigh. "Oh, what's up with all the witnesses going to the jury box?"

He was wearing the talking-to-an-idiot expression on his face again. "Did you listen to anything I said before the trial? Trust in the honesty of the canine spirit? Jury of five? Ring any bells?"

"So *they* will be my jury? They'll vote on if I'm innocent?"

"Yes."

"Yeehaw! I'm home free! They wouldn't vote against me!"

"Just remember that dogs do the right thing. Even when it hurts."

"You mean... You think... Naw, they wouldn't... would they?"

"I never try to second-guess a canine jury."

The bell rang, and we knew the recess was over. We all headed back inside. I wondered what the verdict would be...

"Court is back in session!" yelled the bailiff. The dogs all took their seats. At the prosecutor's table, Nicholas Beales was coiled in his chair, and pointedly avoided looking my direction. He looked only a little worse for the accident.

Judge Scout came out of his chambers, his robes swirling around him. He leapt up to his chair and scowled down at the entire courtroom. "I will not have any further incidents like that in this courtroom. You will show this court, the counsels, and me the respect we deserve." Glaring at Maggie, he continued, "And you, young lady, have done your human friend no favors. We are ending your testimony where we left it. I assume there is no disagreement from either counsel?"

"None, your honor," Hayes and Beales responded together.

"And both parties will stipulate that Miss Maggie has taught the human to play?"

"Yes, your honor." Hayes almost laughed; Beales almost screamed.

Judge Scout gave his next glowering look to me. "And you, sir, will be lucky if Mr. Beales does not file charges against you. I will not tolerate any further exhibitions of this nature. Is that clear?"

Hayes' elbow knocked a "Yessir" out of my lips.

No, this was not good. Not good at all.

"Mr. Beales, do you have any further witnesses?"

"No, your honor, and a good thing, given how my head feels. The prosecution rests its case."

"Mr. Hayes?"

"No witnesses to call, your honor. The defense rests its case." I sure hoped Hayes knew what he was doing.

"Fine, then we'll proceed with closing arguments."

CLOSING ARGUMENTS

Beales strutted—how *does* a snake strut, I asked myself—to the jury box and launched into his closing summary.

"We have here, esssteemed members of the jury, an open-and-shut case. Despite some of the best tutoring by the best teachers that caninity has to offer, a dangerous human, an unworthy human, awaits your judgment. His loyalty did not extend to the very being who *taught* him loyalty. He raised not a finger to save her. His idea of duty did not include calling a doctor for Mr. Snowball as he died on a desolate road. His notion of love went so far as sending cookies, but no further. And did he play? Only when forced to. Fidelity? He was not there even once when his canine companions truly needed him. Each of them faced dire consequences on their own. Alone."

"You have no choice in your verdict. The facts are clear. He is mosssst unworthy of membership in the pack." He confidently slithered back to the prosecutor's table.

Judge Scout nodded to my attorney. "Mr. Hayes. Your closing?"

Hayes rose and approached the jury box. He strutted from one end to the other, looking deep into each juror's eyes, before uttering a word. He knew how to play to an audience. Every eye in the courtroom followed him.

"Members of the jury, the case is not nearly so simple as Mr. Beales would have you believe. He reduces each charge to one event. But this trial is about the entire life of this human, and how he lived it overall.

"As a child, his treatment of Miss Trixie and Mr. Snowball may have been less than admirable, but he was a child. As an adult, he treated Miss Suki, Mr. Angelo, and Miss Maggie with the tenderest of regard. He took the lessons of love and applied them as best he could. He took the daily lessons of play from Miss Maggie and eventually learned to dance naked in the rain. And fidelity? Each rainbow, each sunrise, each sunset, he shared with Angelo on their walks. Everyday walks of exploration and wonder and companionship.

"Is he perfect? No. But who among us is? Given a chance—a chance that only you can give him—he will continue to learn. He will be an example of whom we may all be proud. Someone our pups may one day see as a role model.

"Find this human, this man, worthy. The pack will be better for it." As before, Hayes pulled out a handkerchief and dabbed his eyes. Apparently the snake of a prosecutor was not the only lawyer in heaven well versed in theatrics. Hayes walked back to our table with his tail at half-mast, neither proud nor ashamed.

Once Hayes was seated, Judge Scout turned to the jury and solemnly addressed them.

"The process you are about to embark on is a sacred one. Your decisions will affect not only the life of the defendant, but also the lives of all members of the pack. If you determine he is worthy, his strengths and his weaknesses will become a part of the pack.

"If you find him lacking in the qualities we've examined in this trial, he will bear consequences. But our pack will suffer, too. We will never know his strengths.

"You are to consider only the evidence presented in this courtroom. Though each of you know him in more completeness than was presented, that knowledge is not to be a part of your decision making.

"You are to return a verdict on each of the following attributes: loyalty, duty, love, play, and fidelity.

"When you have completed your deliberations, signal the bailiff, and we will reconvene the court. Godspeed to each of you as you weigh the facts. You hold the fate of a man and your pack in your paws.

"This court is adjourned until the jury has reached a verdict." Judge Scout struck the gavel one time and exited to his chambers.

The five members of the jury were led by the bailiff through a door to begin their deliberations. The prosecutor slithered off to wherever prosecutors slither. The crowd in the gallery wandered through the door at the back of the courtroom, murmuring only when they reached the out of doors.

Hayes put a paw on my shoulder and said, "Let's go for a walk."

We, too, exited through the large door at the rear of the courtroom. For the first time, I noticed the carvings in the door. Canines, mostly, but a few humans too. It was the carving at the center of the door that should have caught my attention before. Larger than the other figures, a solitary dog stood near a creek. Golden rays of light emanated from the dog's head as from a sunset, or maybe a sunrise. The dog was a Border Collie. A Border Collie with exactly the same markings as Angelo's.

"Is that—" I began to ask Hayes.

He nodded. "He's one of the old ones. His soul has been around longer than any of us can remember. You have no idea how surprised we all were when he chose you."

"No more surprised than I was, I'm sure."

Hayes ignored me. "His is a soul that has befriended many of the greatest of your kind. When your Christ spoke with the woman about offering crumbs to the dog beneath the table, that dog was Angelo. While Buddha sat under the banyan tree,

74

Angelo was there to guard him. Angelo walked with Gandhi through the protests in India."

I turned my eyes from the carving as Hayes nudged me toward the outside. "Come on." Through the courtyard and back to the cobblestone street we walked.

"All my life," I began, "I assumed that we humans were the masters and that my dogs were somehow less than me."

"Hogwash. You told yourself that, but you never really believed it. You knew you were equals, that you were in it together, that you were partners. Maybe that's why he chose you."

The sky above us was cerulean blue. It was the first time I truly understood the meaning of that adjective or saw that color.

"I've asked this before, but why do you dogs do it? Why do you weave your fates with ours?"

"Because we need each other. We complete each other. Duty works both ways. Love needs a beloved. Loyalty needs two to be loyalty. Fidelity is nothing without someone to be faithful to. Every dog needs a human, and every human needs a dog."

We walked in silence until the courthouse bell pealed. We turned and walked back without another word.

THE VERDICT

"Thou art weighed in the balances, and art found wanting."
—Daniel 5:27, KJV

After the gallery, Hayes, Beales, and I were all seated; Judge Scout was announced by the bailiff. "All rise!" We did, and then we were seated again. The door to the jurors' deliberation room opened, and the five jurors walked out and into the jury box. The last to be seated was Snowboy.

Judge Scout looked at the jury and asked, "Has the jury reached its verdict?"

Snowboy stood and answered, "Yes, sir, we have."

The bailiff walked to Snowboy, retrieved a sheet of paper from him, and carried it to the judge. Judge Scout looked at it, without expression.

"The defendant will stand to receive the verdict."

Hayes and I both stood.

Judge Scout read the jury's verdict in a plain and solemn voice, "In acts of loyalty, the defendant is found lacking. In display of duty, the defendant is found lacking. In the ability to love and to act on that love, the defendant is found lacking. In recognizing the value of play, the defendant is found lacking. And in the quality of fidelity, the defendant is found lacking. The defendant is found unworthy of pack membership and is unqualified to be a canine."

The air rushed out of my lungs, and the courtroom went black.

WAITING FOR SENTENCING

When I opened my eyes again, I was in a small room with Cowboy. His eyes had never looked bluer. His expression was just as blue, like he'd been kicked when he was down and out.

"I don't suppose you're going to tell me this was all a dream."

"I wish I could, Einstein, but it hasn't been. It's as real as it gets."

"I guess I passed out."

"Yeah, I guess you did. You hit the floor pretty hard, but the doc says you didn't really hurt yourself."

"They have doctors here?"

"The best that dog biscuits can buy."

"You know, I wish Suki had kept her mouth shut. You know, about me loving you."

"I don't think dogs are very good at keeping secrets, and Einstein, you weren't too good at keeping that secret from me, either."

I blushed. "I didn't want to embarrass you. I mean, you're a big tough Marine and all."

"Every tough guy has a soft spot in his heart, too, Einstein."

"So what now, Cowboy?"

"I don't know, Einstein. I guess we wait to see what the sentence is. I'm supposed to let the bailiff know when you are conscious. I'd better call him."

"Before you do. I just want to say one thing, Cowboy. Just one thing. I love you man. I don't know if it's right, or what kind of love, or any of that, but I know I love you, and I hope some way we get to be together, at least for a little while."

"I hope so, too, Einstein. I hope so, too." For only a moment, his hand touched mine.

He rose, opened a door, and signaled to the bailiff. I rose to my feet to see if I could walk. Dammit, I could, despite the dizziness. But whether the dizziness was from the fall I took or the words that I finally said out loud, I really couldn't say.

SENTENCING

The bailiff led me from the small room to join Hayes at the defense table in the courtroom.

The courtroom had begun to fill, not in the orderly fashion I'd seen during the trial itself, but a dog here and a dog there, filling the seats of the gallery at random. Finally the gallery was full. The dogs were more unruly than during the trial, too. There were occasional yips and growls. Not a riot by any means, but it was clear I wasn't the only one feeling tension. I still couldn't believe that my friends would find me guilty, even though they didn't use that word. Lacking. Found lacking. The words echoed in my head.

A door near the jury box opened and my friends filed in. I still thought of them as my friends. I knew their job had been difficult. Duty overruled love, loyalty, fidelity and play. In the pack, duty had to win out, for the good of the pack.

The door to the judge's chambers opened.

"All rise!" the bailiff sung out. At least he sounded happy.

Judge Scout climbed into his chair behind the bench and surveyed the room. His eyes were red. From crying?

He raised his gavel and barely tapped it on the bench. "Order, order." The exclamation points his voice usually carried were gone, and he sounded hoarse.

"The defendant will approach the bench," he finally instructed. Hayes and I walked around the defense table to stand in front of Judge Scout. He peered over the edge of the bench at us. I'd never felt more like a bug under a microscope than at that moment.

Silence stretched out. I heard someone in the gallery cough. The judge broke the hush at last.

"In all my years in this court, I have never been presented with such a predicament as your case presents, Mr. Leland. You have brought into this courtroom the best and worst of humanity and caninity.

"Your kindness and your love have cemented the friendship with your four-legged friends in a bond the likes of which I have only rarely seen before. Their testimony revealed a dedication and loyalty to you that is inspiring.

"And yet, that very dedication is what is most troubling to me. That dedication swayed them to prevaricate, mislead, and very nearly lie in this courtroom. Such perjuries have never been documented in the long history of the canine justice system. Such lies strike at the very foundation of canine ideals.

"Surely you can see the quandary that your case presents. And surely you can see that there is only one reasonable resolution. It is my duty to ensure the safety of the pack, both physically and morally. Your very being and your very life are subversive and a threat to that safety. Above all else, I must guarantee that safety.

"Therefore, with a heavy heart, I sentence you to imprisonment in perpetuity, with as little contact with canines as possible, to minimize your danger to the pack."

There were five gasps from the jury box and another that rose from my own throat. I heard Cowboy sigh from somewhere behind me.

Judge Scout asked the obligatory question, "Do you have any final words?"

I looked him in the eye. I tried to think of something, anything, to say. At last, I mumbled, "Your honor, I'm sorry. All of my life I have been blessed with four-legged friendship. If somehow I endanger that, endanger them, if somehow my transgressions are that serious, then you must lock me away. You must keep them safe..." There were no more words in my brain nor in my heart.

"Bailiff, please see to the human's incarceration." His gavel fell from his grip, and Judge Scout returned to his chambers. The Dalmatian bailiff grabbed me by the scruff of the neck and led me away, through another door. The last thing I saw before that door slammed shut was Angelo. Surrounded by Trixie, Snowboy, Maggie, and Suki, he wept.

10 MERCY

"A dog has the soul of a philosopher."
—Plato

I heard a ring of keys jangling long before I saw the Dalmatian carrying them. He was the same Dalmatian who had locked me in this cell only the day before. Was it really only yesterday? Time seemed to flow at its own pace here, and the night had been the longest I had ever known.

"The judge wants to see you."

"Why?" I was struck by the sullenness that my voice had taken on.

"I just do as I'm told. Wouldn't hurt you none to do the same."

He fussed with the keys and finally opened the cell door. "Follow me," he said in a prison guard voice. He surely must have heard—and maybe told—a thousand jailhouse stories.

Down a long hall we walked. All the cells we passed were empty. I saw the hash marks that prisoners carved in the walls to count their days of imprisonment. That morning, I had carved the first in my own cell.

We came to a gate. He rattled the keys until he found the right one to unlock it. Around a corner, there was a door. The same door I had heard slam behind me yesterday after the sentencing.

Again I found myself in the courtroom. How different it felt, sounded, looked, and smelled now that it was empty. The jury box. The judge's bench. The defendant's and prosecutor's tables. Nearly as empty as my heart felt just now.

My Dalmatian guard opened the door to the judge's chambers, motioned me in with his paw, but remained outside.

"As you requested, your honor. The prisoner. Anything else I can do?"

"That will be all, bailiff," Judge Scout dismissed him. The door closed. Judge Scout looked me in the eye from his comfortable leather chair behind the massive oak desk. He held my eyes for what seemed an eternity. Finally he waved at a chair. "Sit. Stay."

I obeyed.

"No doubt you are wondering why I've asked you here," he intoned as if he'd invited me to an inquisition.

"Well, I—"

"Silence, please. All will be made clear."

He opened a drawer and removed two bones, offering one to me.

"No, thank you, sir."

His arched eyebrows made clear that this was the wrong answer. Reconsidering, I reached the mile from the prisoner's chair to the desk of the dispenser of justice. He nodded approvingly. I held the bone in my hand as I'd once held a cigarette, uncertain what to do with it. Was this the canine equivalent of the last cigarette before an execution?

Again his brown eyes found and held mine until I squirmed. I heard the distant tick tock of a clock.

"I think there may have been an error—a miscarriage of justice—"

I took a deep breath; perhaps the first real breath since I entered his chambers, but I maintained silence.

"Do you remember when you first awoke in this place, when we first met?"

Not trusting my voice, I nodded.

"Do you remember my lesson on imagination? On how if you believe strongly enough, it changes reality?"

Again I nodded. The clock's ticking seemed to grow louder in his long pause.

Without warning, he pounded his bone on the desk. His face was red with anger. "You. Do. Not. Or you have forgotten, or you are stupid, despite your friends' testimony to the contrary."

I looked down at his desk. Near the dent the slamming bone had made was a file. My file. The pages were dog-eared and worn, as if it had been read a thousand times.

"If you did remember, you would understand how this trial came to be—why you were found guilty—and why you were imprisoned!" He was shouting now. My ears burned from humiliation.

Again there was silence. Still that incessant clock ticked. I counted 42 ticks before he spoke again.

"Who do you think created this place?"

My voice sounded Alice-in-Wonderland small when I answered, "God?"

The anger in his face was displaced first by disbelief, then by patience.

"Not literally. Not directly. Let me ask you this: Whose reality is this?"

Even the clock stopped as I considered his question. "Mine?"

He nodded. "And who has the power to create or change reality?"

Where was that comforting tick tock?

I whispered, "I do."

"And what do you think that means?"

I thought for a moment, wanting to give the right answer. "When we die, we go to a heaven that we've imagined, that we've believed in?"

The judge looked at me with patience. "Before and after you die, you are in a place—with characters, with purpose, and even with plot—that you've imagined, that you've believed in. That you *believe* in."

"So, none of it is real?"

"I think we've talked before about this real versus imaginary confusion."

"You spoke of a mistake—"

"Yes, an error. There was an important aspect that *you* forgot to imagine. Surprising, actually, since you offer it so easily to others."

I was stymied. I had no idea what he was talking about.

"As much as I enjoy watching you struggle—it's how we learn the hardest lessons best, I believe—I will spare you."

The clock began its steady tick tock again.

"You forgot to imagine—to believe in—mercy. Forgiveness. The opportunity to move beyond guilt."

"Mercy?"

"Do you think you can imagine and believe in that—for yourself, I mean?"

I closed my eyes and tried. Unworthy—forgiven. Selfish—forgiven. Self-centered—forgiven. Arrogant—forgiven. Was I imagining? Or was this praying?

"That's a good start. I think you're going to need a lot of practice in this lesson. Will you commit to me that you will do this practice?"

I nodded. I answered in my normal voice, "I promise."

"Then you are free to go."

He stared at me with the look of infinite patience in his eyes. Finally, he rose as if to leave.

"Wait—before you go—is there a God?"

He smiled with a patience learned through the centuries. "Someone had to imagine you, didn't he?"

The clock chimed.

"I believe you have an appointment to keep, a destiny to imagine—to believe—to fulfill." Judge Scout turned, his robes flowing like water around him and walked out of the room.

So did I, armed with the idea—no, the reality—of mercy.

11 THE BEGINNING

God give to me by your grace what you give to dogs by nature.
—Mechtilda of Magdeburg,
German hermit and author (1207-1282)

As I stepped out of the venerable old courthouse's door, I felt
for the first time what freedom really meant. Leaving the jail
cell—the cage—behind, yes, but more than that. The sweetness
of mercy after all those bitter years of guilt and hiding. The
contrast couldn't have been greater.

My eyes adjusted to the daylight, and there, in the courtyard,
were my friends.

Angelo was first to greet me. His tail was wagging so hard it
nearly bruised my thighs. He jumped up on me, and his head
pressed against my belly. "Together" was the only word that left
his smiling lips.

"Together. Again." I responded.

He jumped down, I moved on to Snowboy, who offered a shake of his paw and a gruff "Congratulations." His paw stayed in my hand just a moment longer than it needed to.

Suki was next, standing with her paws on my thigh. I bent down to hug her. She whispered, "I love you." I whispered the same words back into her pointy little ears.

Trixie came to stand at my side, her head tilted into my waist and rubbing her nose against me. "I just knew it would turn out all right."

I looked at her. "I'm glad someone was so sure! Hey, what was the book that you put your paw on when you were sworn in?"

"Ah. That was a book sacred to us." She looked at Angelo. "A book that tells the story of a great soul."

Maggie, the youngest of our pack, dropped a tennis ball in front of me. "I brought you a present. I'm glad you're out of the kennel!" She promptly stole the ball back and led the others in a game of rocket chase.

And Cowboy. Cowboy hugged me and planted a kiss on my forehead. If only I'd imagined him just a little shorter. "Hey, Einstein, good to have you back. Real good." And his hug grew tighter before he released me.

There was my attorney next in line. "Hey, old man. Sorry I couldn't do anything to spare you all that, but you know, you make your bed, etc., etc." His paw slapped me on the knee.

"Ouch! Yeah, thanks for everything." He wandered out of the courtyard and down the street, back to his office, awaiting the next call of the court receptionist.

If the others surprised me, nothing could have come as a greater shock than who was last in line. Nicholas Beales, Esq., Bub to his friends, turned his serpentine eyes on me and offered, "Thankssss for the besssst role I've had in agesssss. You have quite the imagination."

"Huh?"

"Yesssss, you wrote my part well."

Of course. I imagined—and made real—even his role in these shenanigans.

He slithered off into the tall grass, awaiting his next performance.

I turned to Cowboy. "Well, what now?"

Concise as ever, he answered, "Soon as those yayhoos get tired of playing chase, we got places to go, people to meet."

For the moment, for *this* moment, I was happy not to move a muscle, not to say a word. Just to be in this pack. *My* pack.

At last the game of rocket chase wore down, and we seven stood facing each other in a circle. After a few moments, without a word, Angelo took off through the gate, and down the street, toward the setting sun. We all followed.

As I passed through the gate, my body felt as if it were having a stroke or convulsions. Smells became three-dimensional. My eyesight changed. Things that moved were very obvious, but objects that were stationary faded into the background. My hearing was more acute and directional. Without a thought, I knew exactly where each bark, each footfall, originated.

The earth beneath my hands felt smooth and warm. My hands? My paws! I looked over my shoulder and saw for the first time my glorious plume of a tail, its fur feathering and blowing in the wind.

A glance at Cowboy showed that he had undergone the same metamorphosis. Our black and white coats glistened in the late evening sunlight. We were truly members of the pack now, for we had been transfigured. We were Border Collies.

Grinning, Cowboy and I ran with the other dogs. We seven, we seven dogs in heaven, were set for adventure.

12 EPILOGUE

For several weeks, Angelo, Trixie, Snowboy, Suki, and Maggie taught Cowboy and me the ropes. We ran together. We hunted together. We played together. The cool, refreshing water of the creek was never far away.

We learned the rules of being in a pack, of how to tell who was the alpha. We learned the responsibilities of leading and following, of hunting and sharing, of working together. These were glorious days for me, and for all of us.

For years, I thought that somewhere in those weeks, we also passed the dividing line between heaven and earth. Now, I see that I was wrong. Another lesson learned: There is no boundary between heaven and earth unless we believe in one.

The days were not always easy. Sometimes what started as play became full-fledged challenges for dominance. Maggie, especially, seemed to delight in the fact that there were two former humans below her in the pecking order.

More than a couple of times, she grabbed either Cowboy's or my hind leg and flipped us on our backs. Still, the pack kept its order. When the play got too rough, Angelo or Snowboy would take the aggressor aside and deliver a quiet lecture, sometimes accompanied with a growl or a nip to the ears.

The alpha, Angelo, was obviously a male, but the females of our group were just as essential to everything running smoothly. Whether removing thorns from paws (those opposable thumbs really would have helped) or soothing the occasionally bruised ego, Trixie, Suki, and Maggie were right there when they needed to be. Their ability to hear seemed stronger than that of us males, too.

Group decision-making was another opportunity for Cowboy and me to learn. Somehow—even after all these years, I don't know how—the entire pack arrived at the same decision almost always at almost exactly the same time.

Almost always. There was a time I saw Trixie and Angelo staring at each other as if they were in an argument, but of course they were communicating telepathically. I missed being able to eavesdrop.

There came an evening when Angelo barked the come-to-counsel call. We all dropped our sticks and tennis balls and whatever we were doing, and ran toward him. A feeling of dread filled my stomach.

He called us to order, and everyone sat in sphinx-like poses, eyes firmly fixed on our leader. He gave a ceremonial howl, and then came straight to the point. Cowboy and I were sitting next to each other, so it was easy for Angelo to focus on us.

"You pups," he spoke in our heads, "have been fast studies. You've learned manners, responsibility, survival skills, camaraderie, just about everything we've thrown at you."

I looked at Trixie, who wouldn't meet my gaze. Cowboy looked at Suki, who was uncharacteristically ignoring him. Maggie stared at Angelo as if she were afraid to look anywhere else. Snowboy simply held his head high, looking for something in the distance. Dread was definitely working its way from my stomach up to my throat. My nose picked up the scent of fear from Cowboy, too.

"And now," Angelo continued, "it's time for you to go out on your own."

On our own. The quiet was broken when Cowboy cleared his throat. Neither he nor I had perfected telepathy, but we were getting better at it. "On our own? We can't all just stick together?"

Angelo weighed his words and answered, "The needs are too great, and there are too few of us. We have a duty, a responsibility to help others. It's not all about fun. It's not always easy."

"We have, however, decided that the two of you should stay together, seeing this is your first assignment."

I felt, but gave no external sign of, relief. I cleared my throat and asked, "But what about all of you?"

"Each of us has our own assignment. I'm going back to comfort a grandma who comforted me once. I'm repaying that kindness." Angelo's eyes glistened as he remembered.

Snowboy volunteered, "I'm going to go protect a boy. Help him grow up."

"L-l-like once you helped me," I stuttered. He nodded.

Trixie, still looking no one in the eye, explained, "I'm going to an old veterans' home, where soldiers think that everyone's forgotten them."

Suki finally looked at Cowboy and said, "I'm going to comfort a mother who lost her son way too early. I think you might know her." Angelo silenced her with a growl.

Maggie dropped a tennis ball—where did she always find them?—and almost pouted. "I'm going to go live with a little girl in the city. Poor thing. Her mother has two jobs and not a lot of time left in her days for love. I'm going to teach her how to play."

"And our assignment?" Cowboy and I spoke with one voice.

Angelo answered, "That's for you two to decide. Nobody gave us our assignments. Well, there were some suggestions, but we chose them."

I'd never heard a dog's voice crack with emotion before, but mine sure did now: "And will I ever see you all again? Together, I mean?"

"That, too, is up to you. Can you imagine—can you believe—that could happen?"

I closed my eyes, and I knew I could.

Both night and silence had fallen on our group. A full moon rose in the east and, without thinking, we all sang—howled, I suppose—our plaintive song, our song of good-byes. After a while, voice after voice dropped out, until only Angelo's deep baritone filled the night air. At last, even he stopped.

We crowded together. Fall was not far off. We did our obligatory three turns and curled up, each touching the others. I wanted to remember this warmth, this symphony of scents, for a very long time.

When Cowboy and I awoke the following morning, we were alone.

13 REPRISE

"Dogs have a way of finding the people who need them, Filling an emptiness we don't even know we have."
—Thom Jones

Cowboy and I found our home, and it wasn't a big surprise that it was with a man who lived alone. An old Marine without family or friends opened his door to us, and that's where we stayed. He didn't talk a lot, at first, but as he realized we weren't going to leave him like so many others had, he opened both his heart and his lips. His southern drawl comforted me, as I imagined that my human voice had once comforted Angelo. Sometimes he sang to us.

He named us. It's a very odd feeling to have someone choose a name for you when you have your own perfectly good name. But that is what humans do. They name everything in their own language, without any regard to the desires of that which is being named.

He called me Tino. He told me, thinking that I didn't understand, that the very first Border Collie he'd ever met was named Tino. He said that Tino was one of the smartest and best-looking dogs he'd ever met, and that I had big shoes to fill. As if I wore shoes.

But when it came to Cowboy, something odd happened. The Marine looked into Cowboy's eyes, and said, "I'm calling you Cowboy. I'm calling you Cowboy because that's what I always wanted to be, and you've got some of that wild west spirit in you."

"Unfair," I telepathically shouted to Cowboy. "Why didn't he name me Einstein?"

Cowboy only snickered.

As we spent more time together, Cowboy and I worked our way through the confusion of love. Just like Suki said, we experimented with all the kinds of love, and at last we found the right mix of ingredients. We cuddled with each other every night.

When the Marine had nightmares, we both slept with him and gave him what comfort we could.

The Marine knew what he was doing when he named Cowboy. Cowboy was a renegade. It was that quality that brought him to an early death. Hell, he probably was just ready to go. In any case, he decided to show off for the Marine, and tried to herd a bunch of elk into a circle. He was doing just fine until one of the bucks got behind him and shoved him down on the ground with his big rack of antlers. I screamed and ran toward him, but I didn't get there soon enough to keep the buck from trampling him. I did bring the buck down, though, and there was plenty of elk meat that winter for both the Marine and me. And so it was just the two of us.

In a way, I was jealous of Cowboy. I pictured him with Trixie, Snowboy, Suki, Maggie, and my beloved Angelo. Lord, how I missed them, even as I knew our time of reunion would come.

As the years passed, I could see the Marine struggling more and more to wake up, but each morning, I put my paw on his shoulder, reminding him it was time for our walk. I struggled, too, with loneliness for Cowboy and with the arthritis that crept into my bones.

It took longer and longer for him to get dressed, and longer still for him to pull his boots onto his weary feet. But we walked. Through rain and snow and hail and summer sun, we walked. He'd talk to me about the flowers we saw, and we'd play the cloud game, where he looked up and saw wondrous things in the blue Colorado sky.

Sometimes he just said the word "Cowboy" and we'd both sit quietly, mourning in our own ways.

Ours was a simple life. Once a month, we'd both climb into his big old Ford truck. He'd coax its tired engine to start, and we'd drive into town. My face hung out the window, catching the wind and the occasional bug. Each time, we'd take a different road into town. On one of those trips, on one winter morning, we drove past the house that I had built so many years ago.

Neither human nor canine lived there now. It stood, but its windows were dirty, and the paint had begun to peel. As we continued down the road, a scent memory came to me… it was almost the smell of Angelo, and almost the smell of a coyote.

Some instinct made me cock my ears to listen, and then I barked. The man looked at me in surprise. My barking grew more insistent, and he finally pulled to the side of the road, at least as far as he could, given the mounds of snow on either side.

"What is it? You smell something? Do you want out?"

He opened his door, and I shot out of the old truck, toward the creek that ran a couple of hundred feet away. He trudged through the snow, following my footprints, and calling my name. "Tino, Tino, wait up, boy!" His voice rang clearly through the cold winter air.

"Tino! Where you goin'?"

I stopped at the creek bank. This is where it all started. Where it all ended. Across the creek, a lone canine stood. His coat was a warm gray, like a coyote's. The white flash on his muzzle and up his forehead was like Angelo's. Like mine. It was his scent I smelled from the road. He howled a hello. I howled back. Our voices mourned those who had come before us, and celebrated those who might come after. The man caught up with me. He looked across the creek in awe.

"I never saw a coyote with markings like that." He looked down at me, as if seeing the white stripe on my nose and forehead for the first time. "One of yours?"

I wished I could answer him aloud. One of my brothers, yes. One of my progeny, no. The Marine moved closer to the edge of the creek bank, and all of a sudden I had a premonition of his falling. A second later, he rolled down the bank toward the creek. His broken leg was bent at the same angle mine was so long ago.

I raced down the bank. I stood above him, as he groaned. For a moment, it was as if I were seeing the world through his eyes, as I remembered my own fall down that very creek bank.

I thought of what I could do. There were no houses for miles and miles around. The old Marine had no phone and was wearing a light jacket. The skies were gray and growing darker. The temperature was dropping.

I knew despair. I knew what Angelo must have felt. And I knew that all I could do was comfort him. I went in search of a rabbit. My last gift to the man who took me in. My last gift, until it was my turn to show him the creeks and the meadows of heaven. And I knew how. I'd learned at the paws of the best.

Dogs who live with lonely men do the most peculiar things.

"Be comforted, little dog, thou too in the Resurrection shall have a tail of gold."
—Martin Luther

BONUS SHORT STORY:
CHRISTMAS WITH A COLLIE

It was Christmas Eve morning in the continent's largest alpine valley. An inch or two of snow had fallen during the bone-chilling night. In the east, a winter sun rose, in glorious pink and gold splendor.

Two sets of tracks were written in the clean white crystals: one of two feet, one set of four. The creators of these winter hieroglyphics were surrounded by the glistening snow. One appreciated the diamonds with his eyes, the other with his nose. The snowfall made for a clean slate upon which the scents of wandering rabbits and packrats stood out clearly.

The man walked slowly. The Border Collie rocketed to and fro, but always kept a watchful eye on his companion. They were on a mission. The man held a pruning saw in one mittened hand.

They passed the cottonwood tree beneath which a coyote was nestled in his den. The Border Collie and the coyote had made their uneasy peace long ago. *Stay away from the chickens and you can have your den.* Some nights, when the moon was full, the dog and the coyote sang their howls in harmony.

Past the road to the mailbox, a road where the dog had warned the man of a rattlesnake the previous summer. On they walked, their noses punctuating the cold air with puffs of steam.

The morning of Christmas Eve day. It had been four years since the man had marked Christmas at all. Four years that he had spent building a house in the middle of nowhere, surrounded by only the neighbors that nature provided.

This year, he was determined to celebrate the birthday of one who had come more than 2000 years earlier. This year, he would carefully unwrap the glass baubles to decorate a tree. This year, he would read the Christmas story aloud, if only for himself and Angelo. Funny to be spending the holy day with a dog whose very name meant "Angel."

He'd spotted the piñon tree that summer on one of their many exploratory walks. It was shaped perfectly. He'd convinced himself that it grew too closely to its neighbors, depriving them of sunlight and precious moisture. Its neighbors would be healthier if he took the tree.

In autumn, when the aspen had dressed in yellow, he had written the owners of the property where the tree stood. They lived somewhere in tropical Florida. They had written back, kindly giving him their permission to cut the tree.

When he got their letter, he and Angelo visited the tree to seek its permission, too. In fact, the man did speak to the tree, telling it of its future, lit by glowing electric lights, and holding the heritage of Christmas ornaments from Christmases long past. The tree offered no response, even when Angelo watered its trunk.

Now, a few days past the longest night of the year, man and dog again sought out that tree. As the sun broke free of the eastern horizon, they saw it, and both paused. In respectful silence, they watched a blue jay alight on the top of the tree. The bird removed a seed from the topmost pinecone on the tree. Seeing the explorers, the jay flew off in a swarm of avian invectives.

The man and the dog stared at the tree. Perfectly symmetrical. Just the right height. The gentle sound of wind rustled its branches. The man dumbly regarded the saw in his hand.

The Border Collie spoke, "It's beautiful, isn't it?"

The man turned to Angelo, unfazed by his words. "It is. Think how beautiful it will be at home."

"You're not surprised I can talk?"

"Surprise was when you showed up at my door. Surprise was the first time I said I needed a hammer and you brought it to me. That you can speak is no surprise at all."

The Border Collie wagged his tail. "Good. I was afraid you would think you were hallucinating."

For a while longer, they appreciated the tree. At last, the man hefted the saw in his hand and began to close in on the tree.

"Wait," Angelo instructed. "Before we kill the tree, I want to tell you a story."

"Wouldn't you rather do that in front of the fire at home?"

"No, I think the story needs to be told right here, right now."

The man found a fallen log and sat down. "So, let's keep it short. I'm getting cold."

Angelo sat down beside the man and put his left paw on the man's knee. "My kind are not known for verbosity.

"Some 2000 years ago, my ancestors were guarding a flock of sheep outside a small town called Bethlehem. This story is passed down from one who was there, one named Micah, and these are his words."

I was young then. My memories, though, I assure you, are accurate. I have compared my recollections of the night with others who were there and we had very little disagreement.

It was snowing lightly. The moon was full. The air was cold. The silence was unbroken as the shepherds watched over the flocks. Even the sheep knew something was about to happen and kept their quiet.

A sound, shimmered through the fields of white, voices yet not voices, glimmered in the chill air. Not two, not twenty, but hundreds in a complex harmony.

At last, one voice rose above the others. The harmonies surrendered to a lone tenor voice that rang out with the clarity of a bell and the richness of a pipe organ.

I saw the shepherds drop to their knees in awe, minding not the snow.

"Arise!" the trumpet like voice admonished them. "Fear not! I bring tidings of great joy for all people. For unto you is born this day in the city of David a Saviour, which is Christ the Lord."

The other voices that were not voices joined again, singing, "Glory to God in the highest, and on earth peace, good will toward men."

All the angels but one left to continue spreading the word. The shepherds departed to visit the newborn King of Kings. They left without a thought for the safety or well being of their flocks, and it was good. The sheep, even the lambs, were safe under our care.

The angel who remained kept watch with us. Mostly he was a quiet sort, though on occasion he did join our frolics. He was fleet of foot, holding his tail high, with his fur flying in the wind. You see, the angel, like us, ran on four feet.

On the day that the shepherds returned, the angel gathered us together to say farewell. His parting words were of instruction: "Today, you have a flock of sheep to guard. These sheep walk on four legs. When the shepherds return, you will have another flock to watch, and these have two legs. Guard them well and teach them well. Your examples of love and fidelity will remind them of the newborn King, who brings the promise of eternal life from his Father."

The sounds of donkeys braying from the trail signaled the shepherds' homecoming. The angel put his